W9-CTS-174

RAGGEDY ANN IN COOKIE LAND.

RAGGEDY ANN
IN
COOKIE LAND

By *Johnny Gruelle*

THE **BOBBS-MERRILL** COMPANY, INC.
A SUBSIDIARY OF HOWARD W. SAMS & CO., INC.
Publishers · INDIANAPOLIS · NEW YORK

To Janet Smith of Cleveland, O. This book is joyfully dedicated.

CHAPTER ONE

THE ICE GROTTO

RAGGEDY ANN and Raggedy Andy turned over and over as they fell. Part of the time Raggedy Ann was on top and part of the time Raggedy Andy was on top. But all the time they were sailing through the air, each Raggedy held the other's hand.

It was quite dark, but that did not worry them for both Raggedy Ann and Raggedy Andy have bright little shoe button eyes. One can see very well with shoe button eyes if one is a rag doll stuffed with nice, clean, white cotton. And, of course, being made of cloth and stuffed with nice clean, soft, white cotton, the Raggedys were not hurt even a teeny-weeny bit when they finally lit with soft *blumps* upon the bottom.

The bottom of what?

That was just what Raggedy Ann wished to know. "Where are we, Raggedy Andy?" she laughed.

"I guess we are at the bottom," Raggedy Andy replied, as he stood up and helped Raggedy Ann to her feet.

"Dear me, yes, I know that, Raggedy Andy," Raggedy

7

Ann laughed. "But where is the bottom and where are we now?"

Raggedy Andy scratched his yarn covered rag head and looked all about him. The two rag dolls stood in a large cavern and all about, as glistening as moonbeams, were shiny things just like icicles.

Raggedy Andy started to walk over to look at one of the icicles, but his feet flew out from under him and he sat down with a bump.

As Raggedy Ann helped him to his feet, Raggedy Andy laughed. "It is as slippery as ice!"

"Indeed it is slippery," Raggedy Ann replied. " 'Cause why? 'Cause, Raggedy Andy, it is ice!"

"And here we are down at the icy bottom of somewhere, and we don't know where," Raggedy Andy said.

"Do you know what, Raggedy Andy?" Raggedy Ann asked, and as Raggedy Andy shook his rag head, Raggedy Ann said, "When we followed that cute little bunny rabbit down the hole, we must have taken the wrong tunnel."

And, of course, that is just what the Raggedys had done.

"Everything is of ice!" Raggedy Andy said as he walked up to one of the large icicles hanging from the high ceiling and snipped off the end.

"Taste it, Raggedy Ann," Raggedy Andy said, as he handed Raggedy Ann the little piece of icicle he had broken off.

"*Mmmm!*" Raggedy Ann said. "It's just like frozen soda water."

Raggedy Ann broke off a piece and handed it to Raggedy Andy who agreed that it was indeed frozen soda water and very, very good.

And, as the Raggedys enjoyed the bits of icicle, they discovered that the white icicles were flavored with vanilla, the yellow ones with lemon, the red ones with strawberry, and the brown ones with chocolate.

Raggedy Ann and Raggedy Andy ran and slid upon the smooth ice floor from one icicle to another sampling them all until they had tried every kind there.

"I guess maybe we had better try to find the door," Raggedy Ann finally suggested.

The two rag dolls walked all around the large grotto, but could discover no door. "I guess we will have to stay here until someone throws us a rope from the hole above," Raggedy Andy laughed.

"And I guess that will be a long, long time," chuckled Raggedy Ann, " 'cause no one knows we are down here."

As there was nothing better to do, Raggedy Ann and Raggedy Andy snipped off a great many pieces of the soda water icicles and sat down upon the floor to enjoy them.

And, being as quiet as two little teeny-weeny mice, the Raggedys heard away off in the distance something going *swish, swish,* and the sound grew louder and louder until the Raggedys saw a cunning little man upon skates coming toward them, *swish, swish.* The Raggedys sat perfectly still and the cunning little fellow skated up to them.

"Hello!" he said. "What are you two doing here?"

"We just fell in through a long slippery hole up above in under the large oak tree," Raggedy Andy replied.

"I don't quite understand how you could fall down through a hole up above down below beneath the oak tree!" the little fellow laughed.

"Perhaps that is because you didn't happen to fall with us, Mister, Mister———" Raggedy Ann hesitated for the little fellow to tell his name.

"Weakie," he said.

"If you had fallen with us," Raggedy Ann continued, "then you would understand, Mister Weakie. You see," she added, "we went down a hole up above and turned the wrong corner and fell down a long chute which was down in under the large oak tree!"

Weakie took off his hat and ran his fingers through his hair just as Raggedy Andy often did when he was trying to think extra, extra hard. "I guess I cannot understand!" he finally laughed.

"Well, anyway," Raggedy Ann said, "we thought perhaps we might have to stay in here forever. We could not find a door, so we just broke off a lot of these lovely soda water icicles and sat down here to enjoy them while we had a thought adventure."

"That was right," Little Weakie said as he gave a stroke with his skates and made a figure eight. "But," he added when he swung in front of the Raggedys again, "you did just the wrong thing."

"Ha, ha, ha!" Raggedy Ann and Raggedy Andy both laughed. "How could we be right if we did the wrong thing, Mister Weakie? Just you tell us that, please."

"Won't you both stand up a moment?" Little Weakie

chuckled. Raggedy Ann and Raggedy Andy tried to stand. Neither one could move!

"There! You see?" Little Weakie chuckled again, "you have eaten so many soda water icicles they have melted and run down through your cotton-stuffed bodies. And now you are frozen to the ice floor. So, you see? While it was right for you not to worry and to enjoy the things you had, it was wrong because you then froze to the ice floor."

"Dear me, suz!" Raggedy Ann sighed. "How shall we ever be able to get up from here? I suppose, Mister Weakie, if you tried to pull us to our feet you would just tear the cloth of our clothing. For cloth tears easily when it is frozen!"

"I'll tell you what I will do, Raggedy Ann and Raggedy Andy," Little Weakie said, "I'll skate to my part of the grotto and bring back a tea kettle of hot water and thaw you out. Just you wait right here; I'll be back soon."

"Indeed, we will wait right here!" Raggedy Ann chuckled 'way down in her cotton-stuffed throat.

Little Weakie skated away as fast as he had come and when he had disappeared, Raggedy Andy said, "Well thank goodness we shall soon be able to get up, Raggedy Ann."

"Indeed you had better be getting up from there!" a loud voice cried from behind the Raggedys. "Now, both of you, get up immediately and leave my soda water grotto." A strange little creature no larger than Raggedy Andy walked around and stood in front of the two dolls.

"If you please," Raggedy Ann said in a very polite manner, "we are frozen to the ice floor and cannot get up, as much as we should like to."

"Then I shall get an ice pick and pick the ice away from you and take you home and make noodle soup out of you," the strange little creature cried as he ran away.

"What a silly thing he must be!" Raggedy Ann exclaimed when the strange little fellow was out of hearing. "Anyone should know that we cannot be used in noodle soup when we are made of cloth and stuffed with clean, white cotton."

"That is quite true, Raggedy Ann," Raggedy Andy agreed. "But this funny creature does not know that and if he puts us into a kettle and tries to make soup of us, then the hot water will take all the paint off of our faces. I guess we had better run and hide."

"Ha!" Raggedy Ann said. "You forget, Mister Raggedy Andy, that we cannot run. And, unless Little Weakie returns before this funny little fellow does, we shall be made into noodle soup. Whee! Isn't that funny? Noodle soup out of two rag dolls!"

Raggedy Andy had to laugh, too, for it was funny to think about even if he did not care to be put into a kettle and stewed.

Presently, however, they heard the skates of Little Weakie, swishing towards them, and they felt very grateful to him.

"You will have to hurry," Raggedy Ann told Weakie. "A moment ago a strange little creature said that he wants to take us home and make noodle soup of us."

"He has gone home to get an ice pick!" added Raggedy Andy.

"Then I shall hurry," Little Weakie said as he poured the hot water around the Raggedys. "It must have been Hookie-the-Goblin who was talking to you. He is a very silly creature to wish to make noodle soup out of two nice rag dolls!"

"We think so, too," Raggedy Ann said as she stood up.

It took more hot water and more time to thaw Raggedy Andy from the ice, and, just as he got to his feet, the steps of Hookie-the-Goblin could be heard as he ran towards them with the ice pick.

My, but he was angry when he saw Little Weakie rescuing the Raggedys, and he cried out, "Here! You wait a minute, Mister Weakie. I want those two to make noodle soup."

"Not today, Mister Hookie-the-Goblin," Little Weakie cried, as he took a Raggedy under each arm and skated away.

Hookie-the-Goblin ran after Little Weakie, and once Weakie said, "I guess I had better put you down and fight with Hookie-the-Goblin and teach him better manners!"

But Raggedy Ann said, "No! I wouldn't fight with him, Weakie. It is wrong to fight unless you have to. I don't believe you'll have to fight Hookie to rescue us."

"I can skate a great deal faster than Hookie can run!" Little Weakie agreed. He skated through a hole behind some large soda water icicles which the Raggedys had missed when they searched for a way out. They looked down a long hall. Along this Little Weakie skated as fast as he could go and close behind him came Hookie-the-Goblin, his feet striking the ice, *clumpity-clump.*

"Oh, dear," Little Weakie cried, "I have taken the wrong hall. And, see, Hookie has closed the ice door! I shall try and skate right through it and break it open. If I can do that, we shall escape."

"I'll tell you what to do, Little Weakie," Raggedy Ann said from under Weakie's arm. "When you get to the ice door, hold Raggedy Andy and me right in front of you. Then, when you strike the ice door, it will not hurt you!"

"But I don't want to give you nice Raggedys such a hard thump," Weakie replied.

"Do not worry about that," Raggedy Ann laughed. "Raggedy Andy and I can be bumped ever and ever so hard and never be hurt the least teeny-weeny bit, for we are soft and loppy and full of cotton!"

"Hee!" Hookie-the-Goblin called behind them, when he saw that Weakie had taken the wrong turn. "Now I shall capture you when you get to the door for it is frozen tight. I'll make noodle soup out of Little Weakie, too!"

Little Weakie skated faster and faster until one could scarcely see his feet so fast they flew, and Hookie-the-Goblin gave another shout as they neared the ice door. He thought surely now he would capture all three. But just as they reached the ice door, Little Weakie held the Raggedys in front of himself and gave a jump into the air.

Crash! He landed right into the center of the ice door. Pieces of ice flew in all directions. Weakie and the Raggedys tumbled through to the other side.

Little Weakie hopped to his feet, and caught up the Raggedys, and away they sped down the icy hall. Hookie-the-Goblin stopped at the door and howled as loudly as a naughty boy who cannot have his own way. "Just you wait!" Hookie yelled. "Just you wait until I catch you."

But Little Weakie did not wait. He sped away leaving a very angry little goblin behind.

When he had skated a long way, Weakie stopped. "I shall have to rest," he explained as he sat down. "Though it's lots of fun to skate, and I like it, I prefer not to be chased!"

"Isn't it funny that Hookie-the-Goblin doesn't skate, when he lives right here in the ice grotto?" Raggedy Ann said.

"Not so very funny," Little Weakie replied. "Hookie-the-Goblin really does not live inside the ice grotto. He lives in the dirt grotto, and there he uses roller skates."

"Listen!!" Raggedy Andy held up his hand. "I thought I heard Hookie's feet thumping the ice. I'll bet a nickel he is still coming after us."

And sure enough, at a turn in the hall, was Hookie coming towards them again.

"We must hurry," said Little Weakie as he caught up the Raggedys. "A short distance from here the ice ends and I will have to take off my skates!" Soon Little Weakie reached the end of the ice and as he stopped and put the Raggedys down he said, "Hurry and help me unfasten my skates. We haven't a moment to lose. The goblin is right behind us."

Raggedy Ann and Raggedy Andy helped Little Weakie unfasten his skates and were hardly finished when Hookie-the-Goblin came running around a bend in the grotto.

"Whoop!" Hookie-the-Goblin cried, when he saw them. "I shall soon have you!"

Little Weakie could not carry the Raggedys now that he was not skating, so the Raggedys and Little Weakie caught hold of hands, and off they all ran as fast as their legs would carry them.

When Raggedy Andy could look back he gave a cry. "Hookie has put on roller skates!"

"Then he will soon catch up with us," Weakie said.

"Can't we hide somewhere?" Raggedy Ann asked.

"If we can outrun Hookie-the-Goblin we could get to a place where we might hide," Weakie replied. "But I am afraid that he will catch up with us before we reach such a place."

Hookie-the-Goblin was gaining upon Little Weakie and the Raggedys at every step and just as they came to a place where the hall divided into two halls, Hookie caught up with them, and grabbed Raggedy Ann's apron.

Raggedy Andy did not know which way Little Weakie intended to run so he started down one hallway while Weakie ran down the other.

When he heard Raggedy Ann cry, "Hookie has caught me!" Raggedy Andy ran back and back came Little Weakie, too.

Raggedy Andy and Little Weakie reached the corner at just the same moment and they bumped together so hard that both of them fell over backwards.

When they got to their feet they saw Hookie-the-Goblin, with Raggedy Ann under one arm, roller-skating away down the hall as fast as he could go.

"Oh, dear!" Little Weakie cried. "Now he will make noodle soup out of Raggedy Ann!"

"Indeed, he won't!" Raggedy Andy cried. "I will run right into Hookie's home and rescue Raggedy Ann!"

Although Raggedy Andy and Little Weakie ran and ran, they could not catch up with Hookie, and at last they saw him skate through an ice door and close it behind him.

It was the door of Hookie's ice home, so Raggedy Andy and Little Weakie sat upon the goblin's front step and felt very, very sad.

CHAPTER TWO

NOODLE SOUP AND COOKIES

*I*T WAS not surprising that Raggedy Andy and Little Weakie felt sad. It is no fun to sit on the cold ice step of a goblin's home, especially if that particular goblin has just captured a very dear friend. No, sir!

"Hookie-the-Goblin will make Raggedy Ann into noodle soup, sure pop!" Little Weakie sighed. "I know Hookie-the-Goblin, and I know that when he says he will do anything mean, he is sure to do it!"

"Of course, it will not hurt Raggedy Ann to be put into a soup kettle and stewed," Raggedy Andy said. "But as you may not know, Weakie, Raggedy Ann has a very nice candy heart sewed up inside her cotton stuffed body, and hot water would surely melt the candy heart to nothing."

"Dear me!" was all Little Weakie could think of to say.

"And this ice door is much too thick for us to break through," Raggedy Andy sighed, "unless we had an ice pick. I do not like to sit here and do nothing while Raggedy Ann is being made into noodle soup, even if rags dolls can't be made into noodle soup."

Kind Little Weakie felt as sorry for Raggedy Ann as Raggedy Andy did, but he could think of nothing to do even though he thought ever and ever so hard.

Raggedy Andy and Little Weakie had been sitting upon the ice step about five minutes when they heard someone coming. Presently a queer little old woman came walking up. She carried a basket, and when she saw Raggedy Andy and Little Weakie she stopped and nodded in a friendly manner.

"Would you like to buy a candlestick?" she asked as she took one from her basket.

"How much are they?" Little Weakie wanted to know. He did not need a candlestick, but he always believed in being polite.

"They are five cents," the little woman answered as she took more of the candlesticks from her basket. "And, if you wish a candle in the candlestick, that will cost one cent."

Little Weakie winked one eye at Raggedy Andy and said to the little woman, "If we should take two candlesticks with two candles in them, how much would that cost?"

The funny little woman thought for a long time, then she took a pencil and figured for a long time on a piece of paper. "Ha!" she said, "if you take two candlesticks with candles in them, it will cost you exactly nothing!"

"Then here it is!" Little Weakie said as he held out his empty hand. "We shall take two."

The funny little woman handed Weakie the two candlesticks with candles in them, then thanking him very kindly, she put the rest of the candlesticks back into her basket and walked away.

"Now," Little Weakie said as he lit the two candles and handed one to Raggedy Andy, "we can melt the ice hinges from the goblin's door and run in and rescue Raggedy Ann."

"We must be very quiet," Raggedy Andy said. "If we

19

melt the hinges we will have to push the door down and that will make a loud noise. Instead, let us melt the ice lock and swing the door open gently so that Hookie-the-Goblin will not hear us."

The flames of the two candles sputtering against the ice lock soon melted it, and pushing the door open very gently, Raggedy Andy and Little Weakie tiptoed through.

"We shall probably find Hookie-the-Goblin in the kitchen," Raggedy Andy whispered to Little Weakie, so they tiptoed down the hall of the goblin's house.

The kitchen door was closed, but Raggedy Andy and Little Weakie could hear the goblin reading from a cook book: "First put a large kettle of water upon the stove to boil and add a pinch of salt; then add other things and boil ten minutes."

Little Weakie and Raggedy Andy could hear Raggedy Ann saying, "Why, Mister Hookie-the-Goblin, you can't make noodle soup out of me. I am nothing but cloth and cotton! You will have to use real-for-sure noodles to make noodle soup."

"Will you please be quiet, Miss Raggedy Ann?" the goblin shouted. "You have made me forget what I have read and now I shall have to read it all over again. What a nuisance you can be!"

"And besides, Mister Hookie," Raggedy Ann said, "if you put me in the hot water it will not hurt me a smidgin, but it may wash all the pretty flowers out of my dress, and it may wash all the paint off my face and the hot water will melt my candy heart with the words '*I love you*' printed on it."

When Hookie-the-Goblin heard this he dropped the cook book and jumped up. "Ha, ha! Raggedy Ann; you are trying to fool me. You haven't a candy heart, I am sure."

"Oh, but really and truly I have," Raggedy Ann laughed. "Just feel here, Mister Hookie."

"Well!" Hookie-the-Goblin cried, "candy heart or no candy heart, I shall make noodle soup out of you just as soon as the water gets hot."

As Hookie caught up Raggedy Ann to put her in the kettle, Raggedy Ann cried, "Here, Mister! You stop that! Besides the water isn't hot enough."

But Hookie would have popped Raggedy Ann in just the same if Raggedy Andy and Little Weakie had not jumped and caught the goblin.

"You will, will you?" Little Weakie and Raggedy Andy cried. "Then we will give you a taste of your own cooking!" And, although the goblin kicked and twisted and tried to bite, Raggedy Andy and Little Weakie lifted him and put him with a great splash into the kettle of water.

It was mighty lucky for old Mister Hookie-the-Goblin that the water was only warm.

Then Little Weakie and Raggedy Andy each caught one of Raggedy Ann's hands and they all ran out of the goblin's house as fast as they could go. "Whee! That's the time we fooled you," they called back over their shoulders, as a sopping wet Hookie climbed out of the kettle.

Down the long hall the Raggedys and Little Weakie ran until Little Weakie had to stop for rest.

Raggedy Ann and Raggedy Andy broke off pieces of the soda water icicles for Little Weakie to eat for they knew that that would rest him.

"If you don't sit down while you eat the soda water icicles you will not freeze to the floor!" Little Weakie suggested.

So Raggedy Ann and Raggedy Andy ate a lot of the icicles while Little Weakie rested.

They were enjoying the soda water icicles so much that they did not hear Hookie-the-Goblin slipping up behind them, until he howled:

"Now I have you!"

"Oh, dear! All three of us have been captured now," Little Weakie cried.

"Yes! I have captured all three of you now!" Hookie-the-Goblin laughed.

"But you will let us finish eating these strawberry flavored icicles, won't you, Hookie?" Raggedy Ann asked.

"Oh, yes," Hookie-the-Goblin replied as he sat down beside Little Weakie. "But you must bring me some of the strawberry flavored icicles to eat while I am waiting to take you all back home with me."

Raggedy Ann and Raggedy Andy hurried to get Hookie some of the icicles for they had both thought of the same thing at the same time.

After Hookie had eaten forty-nine snips of the strawberry icicles he said, "Well, I must take you home now that I have captured you!"

But when he tried to stand up, Raggedy Ann and Raggedy Andy and Little Weakie laughed and laughed, for the wet clothes of Hookie-the-Goblin had frozen to the ice floor, and he could only wiggle and twist and kick about.

"You'll all be sorry for this," Hookie-the-Goblin cried. "Just you wait!"

"We haven't time to wait now," Little Weakie laughed, as he and the Raggedys walked away down the long hall leaving the howling little goblin sitting on the cold, cold ice floor.

The three friends walked and walked through one hall after another until they came to a round door.

"Now what can be in here?" Raggedy Andy wondered.

"The best way to find out is to go inside," giggled Little Weakie as he pushed the door open and put his head inside.

"It's a great big bakery or something!" he said.

"Then let's go inside," Raggedy Andy said. "For if it is a bakery there ought to be a lot of cookies and other good things to eat."

"I guess there are pies and cookies and everything," Little Weakie laughed. "I can smell lots of goodies."

Raggedy Ann and Andy followed Little Weakie into the room, where they found large trays of cakes and cookies and doughnuts and lady fingers all ready to be placed in the ovens, but nowhere could they find anything already baked, though there was icing of different flavors ready to spread upon the cakes and cookies.

"Oh, I'll bet I know," Little Weakie cried. "Any one who comes in here is supposed to bake whatever kind of cookies or cakes or pies he wishes. Then he will have just what he likes best."

"We will bake some and see just how good they are," Raggedy Ann said, as she rolled up her sleeves. "Guess I'll try some of the cookies. Raggedy Andy, if you please, put a bowl of candy icing out on the table so it will be ready to spread on the cookies."

After the pan of cookies was in the oven they had nothing to do but to sit down and wait, and it was while they were waiting that the door was pushed open, and Hookie-the-Goblin appeared.

"Now! Didn't I tell you that I would capture you?" Hookie howled in glee. "I have you and this time I sha'n't sit down on any ice floor and freeze tight, and let you escape."

"How did you ever get loose from the ice?" Raggedy Andy asked.

"I just sat there and howled and howled until my warm tears ran down and melted the ice." Hookie jumped up and sat down upon the table, for Raggedy Ann, Raggedy Andy and Little Weakie were sitting on the only bench in the bakery.

"Whenever you are ready we shall start for my home," Hookie said after a while.

"We are waiting for the cookies to bake," Raggedy Ann

laughed. "And I know they must be done by now." She went to the oven and pulled out the pan, and there were all the lovely cookies baked a golden brown.

"I guess we will have to do without the nice candy on the cookies," Raggedy Ann decided.

"Yes," Little Weakie laughed. "Isn't it a shame that Hookie has to come along and spoil things? But then you know," with a wink at Raggedy Andy, "goblins are such silly creatures!"

"Who says so?" Hookie-the-Goblin cried.

"Who says what?" Little Weakie asked.

"What you just said!" the goblin howled.

"Well? What did I just say?" Little Weakie asked again, and he could scarcely keep from laughing aloud.

"I've forgotten what it was now," Hookie cried. "But it doesn't make any difference. I've captured you, so we shall start to my home!"

"I guess you won't start for a while, Mister Hookie Goblin!" Raggedy Ann laughed. "I believe you are worse than Mister Weakie says you are, for you are sitting in the candy and can't get up!"

Raggedy Ann gave Hookie three of the cookies and she and Raggedy Andy and Little Weakie left him sitting stuck fast in the candy.

Back of the oven-room was another round door; Little Weakie pushed this open and he and the Raggedys walked through and closed the door behind them. Still they could hear Hookie-the-Goblin howling and kicking to get loose.

When the three friends looked around, Raggedy Ann cried, "Oh, dear! We are in the wrong place."

"Indeed, you are!" a deep voice said, and there, coming toward them, was the strangest man they had ever seen.

He was brown: his hands and face and feet and clothes and his hat that was fastened right to his head. He had white lumps for eyes, a red nose, and a red line for a mouth.

When the queer man talked, he did not open his mouth and when he walked towards them he did not move his legs as the Raggedys do. He swung his whole body from side to side, and in this way brought first one foot forward and then the other just as little girls make their stiff-legged dolls walk.

"I guess we have made a mistake," Little Weakie said.

"I guess you have," the man replied in a deep rumble. "This is my place and I never have visitors. Especially real-for-sure people."

"But we are not real-for-sure people," Raggedy Ann told him. "Raggedy Andy and I are only rag dolls, and Mister Weakie here is not a real-for-sure person like people who live up on top of the earth."

"It does not make any difference what Mister Weakie is, I can see that all of you are eating cookies right now, and it makes cold shivery crumbs run up and down my back. I will put you all through the great roller. Then you will be sorry that you came in here."

"We are sorry now," Raggedy Ann hastened to say. "Just let us go and we will leave the way we came in."

"That I cannot do!" the brown man said. "That door opens only from the other way, and you cannot open it from this side. And besides, you must go through the great roller." And touching a button, the strange brown man started the great rollers moving, and caught hold of Raggedy Ann.

"You may go first," he said, as he started to lift Raggedy Ann into the rollers. But Little Weakie, running from behind, gave the brown man a great thumping push, right in the middle of his back.

With a loud *crack*, the man broke in two and fell to the floor. "Why, he's nothing but a cookie man!" Raggedy Ann exclaimed. "His eyes and nose and mouth are just candy icing!"

CHAPTER THREE

THE COOKIE PEOPLE

THE cookie man lay without moving upon the floor after Little Weakie broke him into two pieces.

"He looks as though he had been made of chocolate dough," Raggedy Andy said.

"Why wouldn't it be a good plan to break him into small pieces and put him in our pockets to nibble on when we leave here?" Little Weakie asked.

"Oh, dear me!" Raggedy Ann cried. "We mustn't eat the poor cookie man. Even if he was cross to us, he may have lots of fun doing the things he likes to do. No. Instead of breaking him into pieces to nibble on, let's see if we can patch him together with dough and icing. Maybe he will be all right."

So Raggedy Andy and Little Weakie hunted around until they found a jar of molasses and a box of little colored candies.

"We can paste him together with the molasses, and we can make his brown clothes much prettier by pasting the colored candies on his suit," Raggedy Ann said.

"Raggedy Ann always thinks of the nicest things to do for others," Raggedy Andy told Little Weakie. "I suppose it is because she has a candy heart."

Raggedy Ann took a brush and put molasses all around the broken parts of the man's back, then she painted his clothes with the molasses and placed the pretty colored candies in lovely patterns.

"Now doesn't he look much better?" she asked.

"He looks good enough to eat," Little Weakie said.

"Why doesn't he come to life now that he is mended?" Raggedy Andy wondered.

"Perhaps he has to be standing up," Raggedy Ann replied.

So Raggedy Andy and Little Weakie lifted the cookie man to his feet, and watched him roll his candy eyes.

"What happened?" he finally asked.

"I broke you in two," confessed Little Weakie. "But we have fixed you up better than new with molasses."

The cookie man walked to a looking glass and admired his new suit. "My!" he said. "You have fixed me up so nice, I am afraid my wife will not know me! Thank you, ever and ever so much. Now you won't have to be put through the rolling machine, because I know you are nice, kindly people!

"I want to take you home with me and have you meet Mrs. Cookie and my two children!" Mr. Cookie said.

"We should love to meet them," Raggedy Ann laughed. "I am so glad we mended you."

"And I am very glad, too!" The cookie man chuckled deep down inside his chocolate suit. "When you pushed on my back and cracked me in two, I thought to myself, now I shall never be able to get up and go home to see my cookie family any more. I shall just have to lie here forever and ever."

"I wanted to break you in pieces to put in our pockets

so that we could nibble upon you as we walked along," Little Weakie told the cookie man.

"My goodness! I am so glad you did not do that, though I really am made of nice chocolate dough."

"I love chocolate cookies," Little Weakie said.

"Maybe we had better be going." The cookie man seemed a bit nervous.

"Little Weakie will not nibble you even a teeny-weeny bit. Will you, Little Weakie?" Raggedy Ann asked, to make Mr. Cookie feel better.

"No, indeed," Little Weakie replied as he patted the cookie man upon his shoulder. "Please don't give it a single thought. We are friends, you know."

"Isn't that nice?" the cookie man said. "I am delighted and I shall love you all, I am sure. You know," he said in a whisper, as if it were a great secret, "I have a raisin heart, so that I really and truly can love you!"

Mr. Cookie led the way down a long hall and opened a door. This door led right into a lovely little garden. In the middle stood a cunning house, made of cake and covered with cream colored icing. The roof was red icing, and the chimney was white icing. All about the pretty house were cookie flowers covered with colored icing.

Even the little walk leading up to the house was made of candied icing.

"What a sweet place," Raggedy Ann exclaimed.

Two little cookie children came out to meet the cookie man, and beside them came a cookie dog with raisin eyes.

"These are my cookie children," Mr. Cookie said. "Little Lemon Cookie—that's my little boy's name—fell from a cookie tree the other day and broke off one of his legs."

Our friends were sorry to see that little Lemon's leg had indeed been broken off, and that he had a piece of stick for one leg.

"I shall try and fix him after a while," Raggedy Ann thought.

"And here is Mrs. Cookie," Mr. Cookie said as he led the way into the cake house. Every one sat down in cookie chairs covered with icing while Mrs. Cookie finished getting dinner.

Mr. Cookie told Mrs. Cookie how nice his new friends had been to him, and of course, Mrs. Cookie was surprised and pleased to see how lovely Mr. Cookie's suit looked with the candy trimming on it.

It was a lovely dinner, for Mrs. Cookie had baked a chicken, nice and brown. It wasn't a real-for-sure chicken. It was a cake chicken covered with maple-walnut and chocolate icing to make it look real. And, it was stuffed with chopped cherries and pecan nuts. The gravy for the chicken was chocolate ice cream, just soft enough to pour over it.

The Raggedys and Little Weakie enjoyed the dinner very, very much for it had been almost an hour since they had eaten anything. And then they had had only eleven cookies apiece, and those did not have icing on them. So they were quite hungry.

"I don't know when I have enjoyed such a lovely dinner," Raggedy Ann told Mrs. Cookie when they had eaten until they felt drowsy.

"It was much nicer than nibbling Mr. Cookie," Little Weakie said.

"I am glad that you didn't break Mr. Cookie up and nibble on him!" Mrs. Cookie laughed. "For when a Cookie person is broken up, it is just as though some one had torn Raggedy Ann or Raggedy Andy to pieces!"

"Indeed, you are quite right, Mrs. Cookie," Raggedy Ann said. "And that reminds me that little Lemon Cookie has to thump around upon a stick for one of his legs. Wouldn't it be much nicer if he had a cookie leg?"

"Oh, yes, it would, Raggedy Ann!" Mrs. Cookie replied as she wiped a sugar-water tear from her icing eye. "But we do not know what to do about it. We have no cookie doctor living near us who can fix it."

"Have you some flour and sugar and baking powder and lemon flavoring?" Raggedy Ann asked.

"Oh, yes! I have everything anyone needs to make cookies or cakes with."

"Then," said Raggedy Ann as she rolled up her sleeves, "I shall make little Lemon Cookie a new leg. That's what!"

"Dear me!" Mrs. Cookie exclaimed. "I just remembered that I'm all out of lemon flavoring. Now we can't make little Lemon a new leg!" And she sat down in a rocking chair and cried so hard, Raggedy Ann thought Mrs. Cookie's face would melt all down her dress.

But Raggedy Ann hurried to her and said, "Never mind, Mrs. Cookie, we will bake a vanilla leg for little Lemon. It may make him walk funny with one lemon and one vanilla leg, but it will be better than a stick leg I am certain!"

Mrs. Cookie dried her icing eyes and in a short time she and Raggedy Ann had a nice cookie leg made just the right size for little Lemon.

Then, because Raggedy Ann had a lot of dough left, she made little Strawberry (that was the little cookie girl's name) a nice little vanilla kitty.

When the cookie leg and the cookie kitten had baked long enough they were taken from the oven. The leg fitted little Lemon very nicely and he jumped about and was very happy when the leg was fitted to him.

Then Raggedy Ann put white icing on the kitty for spots and red cinnamon drops for eyes. It was a lovely cookie kitten and little Strawberry was very happy, too. It was great fun to see the stiff-legged puppydog and the stiff-legged cookie cat playing together. They fell down often, but they seemed to enjoy romping together as much as real-for-sure dogs and kitties. And when a little chocolate cookie mouse ran from a hole in a closet and scampered across the room, the cookie kitty caught it and ate it in a twinkling.

"She is a fine cookie mouse catcher!" Raggedy Andy laughed.

Mr. Cookie took Raggedy Andy and Little Weakie about the garden and showed them the cookie turnips and cake cabbages and other cookie vegetables sticking up from the brown-sugar ground. "If we had some cookie chickens and cookie ducks and pigs and cows we should have the nicest farm in the whole world, I guess," Mr. Cookie said.

"Let's get Raggedy Ann to make some," Raggedy Andy suggested.

"That would be very nice," Mr. Cookie agreed. "But she has already done so much, I would not care to ask her to do more."

"You do not know Raggedy Ann as well as I do," Raggedy Andy laughed. "I shall ask her, for I know that when Raggedy Ann makes any one happy by doing something for them, then she gets the most fun out of life."

Raggedy Andy ran into the house, and soon came out again. "Raggedy Ann said that she would start right away, Mr. Cookie. And I'll bet in an hour you will have the nicest cookie animals you have ever seen."

"I'll bet so, too, Raggedy Andy," Mr. Cookie laughed. "Because I have never seen any."

Then he took Raggedy Andy and Little Weakie to the soda water spring and while they drank soda water, they watched the cookie fish swimming around, down in the magic water.

"What do you feed the cookie fish?" Little Weakie asked.

Mr. Cookie laughed so hard he shook three crumbs from the end of his nose. "We do not feed them at all, Little Weakie," he replied. "Mrs. Cookie made them of cookie dough and little Lemon and Strawberry put them in the spring. They just drink soda water all day long and of course they never get hungry for anything else."

"I was thinking of catching one and tasting it!" Little Weakie said. "But if they belong to the cookie children, then I won't because it would be wrong to take them."

"Wrong to take what?" a loud voice asked right behind Little Weakie.

"Why, wrong to take the cookie fish out of the soda water spring," Weakie said, and turning about whom should he see but Hookie-the-Goblin standing there staring at him with large green eyes.

"Dear me!" Raggedy Andy cried. "Why don't you run on home and stop bothering us, Hookie-the-Goblin?" Raggedy Andy almost had to laugh, for the Goblin was rolling his large eyes round and round in his anger.

"Do you know what?" Hookie-the-Goblin howled much louder than was necessary.

33

"No! What?" Little Weakie demanded.

"You fooled me the last time, Mister Weakie and Mister Raggedy Andy, so now I have made up my mind that I shall not be fooled again!" Hookie-the-Goblin stamped his foot just like a naughty child who is angry. "How can you expect me to make noodle soup out of you when you are always fooling me and escaping?"

"Isn't he the silliest goblin you ever saw?" Little Weakie asked the cookie man. "Anyone would know that neither Raggedy Ann, nor Raggedy Andy nor I would wish to be made into noodle soup. Only noodles wish to be made into noodle soup. So there, Mister Hookie!"

Hookie-the-Goblin howled ever so much louder than he had before and made a spring towards Little Weakie. "I'll take you home with me!" Hookie cried. Little Weakie called, "Help!" But Hookie-the-Goblin had caught him.

Raggedy Andy started to roll up his sleeves to help Little Weakie escape, but before Raggedy Andy could take three steps towards Little Weakie, the brave cookie man had hit the goblin so hard with his cookie arm that the goblin fell backwards into the soda water spring.

"Run for the house," the cookie man cried, "before Hookie can climb out of the soda water!"

And they were inside and had the door locked before Hookie-the-Goblin could catch them.

CHAPTER FOUR

HOOKIE-THE-GOBLIN'S REVENGE

"MERCY sakes!" Raggedy Ann cried as Raggedy Andy, Little Weakie and the cookie man came running into the house and locked the door behind them. "Whatever is the trouble? If you jump about and jar the floor so you'll make all my cake dough fall and the nice cookie animals I'm baking will be flatter than pancakes!"

Just then Hookie-the-Goblin, his clothes all wringing wet with cold soda water, came running up the candy icing walk.

"Open the door!" he cried as he thumped his fists upon the candy icing door.

"Don't pay any attention to him," Mrs. Cookie said. "Maybe he will go away."

Hookie-the-Goblin, however, did not intend to leave. He was very angry at the cookie man for upsetting him in the cold soda water spring. "Just as soon as I catch the cookie man, I shall make Washington pie out of him. That's what I'll do!" he shouted through the keyhole.

35

"Oh, look!" Raggedy Andy cried as he heard a thump upon the floor and looked around: "The poor cookie man's arm has fallen off. He must have cracked it when he thumped Hookie so hard!"

"Goody! Goody! Gouch!" Hookie-the-Goblin howled through the keyhole. "I'm glad of it, and just as soon as I catch him, I shall break off every one of his cookie arms and legs. Even his cookie head!"

"You should be ashamed of yourself, Hookie-Goblin!" Raggedy Ann called back. "Besides, I shall soon fix the cookie man's arm in place with nice molasses, just as good as new!"

And Raggedy Ann did. It took her only three minutes.

All this time, Hookie-the-Goblin was pounding and thumping upon the door with all his might.

"It's all Raggedy Ann's fault," he cried through the keyhole when he stopped to rest.

"Silly!" Raggedy Ann replied.

"I'll just sit here upon the doorstep until you get so hungry you have to come out," Hookie told them as he sat down.

"Let him sit as long as he likes," Raggedy Ann whispered to the rest. "For the longer he sits in his wet clothes the harder he will stick when he tries to get up again!"

So while they waited for Hookie-the-Goblin to stick to the doorstep, Mrs. Cookie stuffed another cake chicken with chopped raisins and chopped nuts and ice cream and served it to every one, even the new little cookie kitten with the red cinnamon eyes. And while they enjoyed their meal, they had to laugh at Hookie-the-Goblin sitting out in front howling until he finally went to sleep.

"We'll just let him sleep," Raggedy Ann whispered. "Then when he is stuck tight, we can tie him and carry him home, and he won't bother us again."

It really seemed as if Hookie would sit there long

enough, for our friends could hear him snoring just like this: "Yeeshuff! Yeshuffooo!" He gave a little whistle at the end of each snore.

It sounded so funny that little Strawberry, the cookie girl, began giggling, and this made little Lemon, the cookie boy, giggle and that started Raggedy Ann and Raggedy Andy and the cookie man and lady giggling too.

And they all giggled so much that the little cookie dog began to bark.

Now cookie dogs do not bark like real-for-sure puppy-dogs who eat bones and fried potatoes and things like that. Cookie dogs bark more like this: *"Skuboo! skuboo!"* It sounded as if the cookie puppydog was trying to count up to one hundred, he barked so long. Finally it awakened Hookie-the-Goblin.

"Dear me, suzz! What kind of creature can that be?" Hookie asked himself aloud. He had never heard a cookie dog bark before. Very few people have. Hookie was frightened.

"I believe I had better run home and come back some other time," he said to himself as he tried to get to his feet.

But the harder he tried to stand up the tighter he stuck to the candy doorstep. Hookie pulled and pulled. Suddenly there was a loud *pop* and all the candy nails came out of the candy board step. Hookie flew into the air and turned over three times. Then, with the doorstep hanging to him and thumping him at every step, Hookie-the-Goblin raced across the yard and jumped the garden wall.

When the Raggedys and their friends heard Hookie running away, they opened the door and shouted and laughed, and the cookie puppydog ran after Hookie and barked in his funny cookie dog bark. The goblin who never once looked behind thought that some strange creature was after him, hitting him each time the doorstep banged his back.

38

When the cookie puppydog had chased the goblin far enough, he came back wagging his cookie tail so hard it broke off close to his body.

"Now I shall have to mend his tail," Raggedy Ann declared as she picked up the puppydog's cookie tail and fixed it to his body with sticky molasses.

"Now do not wiggle, or waggle your tail until you are certain it is quite dry!" Raggedy Ann advised him.

"Let's take a walk down to the candy bridge and watch the soda water splash over the rock-candy stones," the cookie man suggested.

"You may all go and I will stay and watch the things I have in the oven," Raggedy Ann said. But Raggedy Andy said, "No, Raggedy Ann. You haven't seen as much around the cookie place as I have. You go with them and I will watch the things in the oven and take them out when they are done."

And that is why Raggedy Andy was the only one at the cookie house when Hookie-the-Goblin returned.

Raggedy Andy had been sitting by the oven so long he had almost gone to sleep when he suddenly felt that something was wrong. Raggedy Andy jumped to his feet and pulled open the oven door.

A great cloud of smoke came pouring out. It did not get into Raggedy Andy's eyes, for Raggedy Andy's eyes are made of shoe buttons.

Raggedy Andy reached in and pulled out the pan of burning cookie chickens and ducks. Through the open door Raggedy Andy threw the burnt cookies, just as Hookie-the-Goblin started to run in.

One of the cookie chickens stuck right to Hookie's long nose.

With a loud howl, Hookie turned, and running as fast as he could scamper, disappeared behind the cookie woodshed.

When Raggedy Andy looked into the oven again, he found that the cookie chickens and ducks were the only ones which had burnt, so he pulled out the cookie cow and the cookie pigs and put them on the table to cool.

"When Raggedy Ann returns, she can put candy eyes in them and they will be alive," Raggedy Andy told himself. Then he leaned back in his chair and waited for the others to come home.

"What in the world have you been doing, Raggedy Andy?" Raggedy Ann wanted to know when she and her friends returned.

"I guess I must have fallen asleep!" Raggedy Andy replied. "And when I found the cookie chickens and ducks were burning, I threw them out the front door."

"And Hookie-the-Goblin came running by us lickety-split," Little Weakie laughed. "He had a cookie chicken hanging on his nose. You should have seen him run!"

"Then I must have been entirely asleep, for I did not see Hookie at all," Raggedy Andy said.

Mr. and Mrs. Cookie were so pleased when they saw the nice cookie cow and the fat cookie pigs, they laughed with pleasure. Then when Raggedy Ann put lovely candy eyes in the cookie animals and stood them upon their feet the cookie cow said, *Mooo!* in a soft, doughy tone, and the cookie pigs grunted softly. Raggedy Ann and Raggedy Andy, Little Weakie and the cookie family were all pleased and patted the cookie animals as they walked out into the garden.

"A-ha!" Hookie-the-Goblin cried as he came jumping over the candy fence. "Just you show me Raggedy Andy! Just you show him to me! He is the one who threw the hot, burnt cookie duck on my nose. I shall soon make him into noodle soup."

"It wasn't a cookie duck," Little Weakie said. "It was a cookie chicken. We saw you running with it hanging to your nose. My! You looked funny!"

"Anyway, I shall capture Raggedy Andy and take him home with me; then you will never see him again!" Hookie howled.

But, Hookie-the-Goblin was very much mistaken, for as he started towards Raggedy Andy, the cookie cow rolled her candy eyes and said, *Mooooo!* ever so gently. She must have been fooling, for she raised her head and scooted Hookie across the garden so fast his feet scarcely touched the ground. Then, when she got him near the candy fence, she kicked up her heels, and with a toss of her head, threw the Goblin right over the candy fence into the blackberry bushes. Then the cookie cow walked back toward her friends with a smile upon her face as much as to say, "Wasn't that fun?"

"Just you wait!" Hookie howled. "I will be back again; then you had better watch out."

"Ha! What will you do?" Raggedy Andy wanted to know.

"You'll soon find out!" Hookie-the-Goblin cried.

"Really, he is the most disagreeable person I ever saw," Little Weakie said. "Let's forget all about him."

"That is the best thing to do with disagreeable people!" Raggedy Ann agreed. "Let's all go into the house. I want to make more nice cookie chickens and ducks for Mrs. Cookie."

So all except little Strawberry and little Lemon went into the cookie house. They stayed out in the garden to pick a bouquet of candy flowers for the supper table.

Raggedy Ann had just put the dough for the cookie ducks and chickens in the oven, and Mrs. Cookie had just placed a lot of maple nut sundaes on the table, when they heard a cry from the garden.

The cry came from little Lemon, the cookie boy.

Little Strawberry could not cry because Hookie-the-Goblin had his hand over her mouth and was running away with her.

"Ha, ha, ha!" Hookie called back over his shoulder. "I told you that I would get even."

"After him!" Little Weakie cried as every one ran to the door.

But when Raggedy Ann and Raggedy Andy and Little Weakie and the cookie people all reached the door at the same time, they squeezed together so tightly, Mr. and Mrs. Cookie were broken right in half and Little Weakie stepped upon Mr. Cookie's foot and broke that off, too.

"Dear me!" Raggedy Ann cried, when she saw the damage, "we can never leave the nice cookie people in this fix. They will have to be mended!"

"While you mend them, Little Weakie and I will chase Hookie-the-Goblin and try to rescue little Strawberry," Raggedy Andy said.

"And I shall go with you!" little Lemon cried, for he was a brave little fellow.

"I hope Hookie does not get hungry and begin nibbling on the sweet little cookie girl," Raggedy Andy said as they ran after Hookie.

"I hope that, too!" Little Weakie replied. "But he may nibble her. It was all I could do to keep from nibbling her

myself when I got hungry. I am very fond of strawberry cookies. But of course, I wouldn't think of really doing such a thing, though!"

"Of course not!" Raggedy Andy agreed.

After Hookie-the-Goblin had run a long way, he grew tired and sat down to rest. "My, I am hungry!" he said aloud. Little Strawberry did not say anything for if she had it might have reminded him that she was a cookie child, and then he would start nibbling her. And *that* would not be any fun for little Strawberry at all.

The longer Hookie rested, the hungrier he became. "If I don't eat something pretty soon, I don't know what I shall do," he said.

By this time Raggedy Andy, Little Weakie and Lemon had come in sight. They saw Hookie sitting down to rest.

"We must slip up quietly behind him," Raggedy Andy whispered to the others. "Then we shall all jump out suddenly and yell as loud as loud can be. Hookie will think it is a wild hooligooly-or-something, and before he has time to think, we can pick up little Strawberry and run home with her."

The goblin was so busy thinking how hungry he was, he did not hear Raggedy Andy, Little Weakie and Lemon until they jumped out and yelled as loud as they could.

Hookie thought it *was* a hooligooly-or-something. He jumped up from where he sat and ran eighty-five feet before he stopped. Then, of course, it was too late.

Raggedy Andy had picked up little Strawberry and was running towards the cookie home.

When Hookie-the-Goblin saw that he could not catch up with Raggedy Andy, Little Weakie and Lemon, he sat down and howled and cried until his nose had turned a bright red.

CHAPTER FIVE

SNITZNOODLE TO THE RESCUE

RAGGEDY ANN had the cookie people all nicely mended by the time Raggedy Andy and Little Weakie returned with the cookie children.

"We may expect Hookie-the-Goblin any minute," Raggedy Andy told the cookie people. "A mean person like the goblin will just keep on being mean and disagreeable. If he but knew it, he is only making himself more and more unhappy."

Mrs. Cookie went to the cupboard and brought out two cookie medals. They were covered with nice white icing.

"These are bravery medals," Mrs. Cookie said as she pinned one on Little Weakie and one on Raggedy Andy.

Raggedy Andy and Little Weakie did not want medals for being brave but they did not tell Mrs. Cookie so, for she thought they would want everyone to know how brave they had been. Being just a cookie woman, Mrs. Cookie did not know that really brave people do not care to brag about their bravery.

"Anyway," Little Weakie thought, "if we get hungry at any time, we can eat the candy-covered cookie medals."

Raggedy Andy and Little Weakie went outside to walk around while Mrs. Cookie and Raggedy Ann fixed more maple nut sundaes. The others had melted. And just as they turned the corner of the house, who should they meet but Hookie-the-Goblin. With him was a Snitznoodle.

"I've brought the Snitznoodle with me so that I can capture you both!" Hookie cried, after he had introduced the Snitznoodle to Raggedy Andy and Little Weakie. "I'll capture Raggedy Andy, and the Snitznoodle shall capture Little Weakie."

Then he caught Raggedy Andy by the arm and the Snitznoodle caught Little Weakie by the arm.

"Wait a moment!" the Snitznoodle exclaimed. "What is this I see pinned upon Little Weakie's breast?"

"That is a medal for bravery," Raggedy Andy told the Snitznoodle, for little Weakie was too modest to say anything himself.

"Ha! then you won't catch me trying to capture him," the Snitznoodle said. "Any one with a bravery medal pinned upon him might be too hard to wrestle."

"Nonsense!" the goblin cried. "But if you are afraid to capture Weakie, then you may capture Raggedy Andy and I shall capture Weakie."

"But Raggedy Andy has a medal pinned upon his breast, too," the Snitznoodle said.

"I have a good notion to thump you," Hookie yelled at the Snitznoodle.

And the notion pleased the goblin so much that he actually did thump the Snitznoodle hard. The Snitznoodle did not like it at all, but he asked immediately, "Have you a bravery medal, Hookie-the-Goblin?"

"No, I haven't, silly," the goblin replied as he gave the Snitznoodle another thump much harder than before.

"Then take that!" the Snitznoodle cried as he gave the

JONNY GRUELLE —

47

goblin such a thump that it sent him head over heels. "And never ask me to help you again." So the Snitznoodle took Raggedy Andy's arm and Little Weakie's arm and walked with them to the cookie house.

"I wouldn't be a mean old goblin for anything," he said. "I'd much rather be a Snitznoodle."

"So would I," both Raggedy Andy and Little Weakie said, for they had liked the Snitznoodle from the very first.

Raggedy Ann and the cookie people were surprised to see Raggedy Andy and Weakie with a strange creature.

"Who in the world can it be?" wondered Raggedy Ann.

"I can't tell you, my dear," Mr. Cookie said. "He looks very hungry, though. I hope he won't eat little Strawberry and little Lemon!"

"Oh, I don't believe he will do that!" Raggedy Ann laughed. "Little Weakie and Raggedy Andy would never bring him to your house if he were rude enough to eat any of you."

Just then Raggedy Andy and Little Weakie walked in.

"Here's a new friend," they said. "This is Mr. Snitz-noodle."

The Snitznoodle had very nice manners; he took off his hat and shook hands with Mr. Cookie, and made a nice bow to Mrs. Cookie and Raggedy Ann.

"What sweet children you have, Mrs. Cookie," he said. This made Mrs. Cookie very nervous, and so Raggedy Ann hastened to take a cookie chicken and hand it to the Snitznoodle.

The Snitznoodle turned the cookie chicken over and over in his hand and asked, "What shall I do with it?"

"You may eat it if you wish," Raggedy Ann said. "Mrs. Cookie is afraid you may be fond of cookies and eat her cookie children."

The Snitznoodle laughed and handed the cookie chicken back to Raggedy Ann. "Never fear. I shall not eat the sweet little cookie children. In fact, I shall not eat the cookie chicken, either!"

"We have plenty," Raggedy Ann told him.

"Yes," I see that you have," the Snitznoodle replied. "But you know, I never eat anything but wind sandwiches."

"Wind sandwiches?" Raggedy Ann asked.

"I am very fond of them," the Snitznoodle said. "And, as they cost nothing, it keeps my board-bill down to a small amount each month."

"I've never heard of wind sandwiches!" Raggedy Andy said.

"Neither have I," a loud voice at the door cried.

It was Hookie-the-Goblin, and he held a large stick in his hand.

"Excuse me a moment," the Snitznoodle said to Mrs. Cookie and Raggedy Ann and, walking to the door, the Snitznoodle gave the goblin six hard thumps, one after the other, so fast it sounded like a drum.

"And don't let me catch you around here again," the Snitznoodle yelled, as Hookie ran out of the yard.

The Snitznoodle came back into the house. "That goblin gets on my nerves," he said. "But never mind. I'm going to show you how to make wind sandwiches. Then if Raggedy Ann and Raggedy Andy and Little Weakie ever get hungry they can find supplies almost anywhere."

The Snitznoodle took a knife from his pocket. "See?" he said. "First I cut two thin slices of air. And then I spread a lump of soft wind on each slice of air and place them together and I have a nice wind sandwich."

Raggedy Ann and Raggedy Andy and Little Weakie tasted the Snitznoodle's wind sandwich, but they did not think it very good.

Mrs. Cookie brought an ice cream cone and handed it to the Snitznoodle. "Try this!" she said.

When the Snitznoodle tasted the ice cream cone, he said, "My! That is ever so much better than a wind sandwich!" And Raggedy Ann and Raggedy Andy and Little Weakie laughed and said that they thought so, too.

The Raggedys found the Snitznoodle a very kindly creature, even if his neck was long. And after the cookie people found that the Snitznoodle would not nibble their children, they liked him as well as the Raggedys did.

Mrs. Cookie gave the Snitznoodle another ice cream cone and then a cookie chicken filled with chopped nuts and chocolate ice cream.

When the Snitznoodle tasted these good things he said, "Mrs. Cookie, I never knew there was such good food in the whole world. So, instead of going back to my stump home and living on wind sandwiches, I shall come and live with you nice people."

"We'll love to have you!" both Mr. and Mrs. Cookie said, for they had seen how hard the Snitznoodle had thumped the goblin, and they thought it would be well to have a brave Snitznoodle about the place to protect them.

"Yes, sir!" the Snitznoodle cried. "I shall run home and get my nightie, and I'll be right back." Then he shook hands with everyone and tipped his hat many times and ran down the candy walk and jumped the fence.

"Isn't he a nice creature?" the cookie man asked.

"Indeed, he is," Raggedy Ann agreed. "I'll bet that Hookie-the-Goblin will not come to your place very often if the Snitznoodle is here."

"Oh, dear!" Mrs. Cookie cried, as she ran to shut the door, "here comes the goblin right now. What shall we do?"

"We shall shut all the doors and lock them, and when the Snitznoodle returns and sees Hookie, he will give him a few more thumps," Raggedy Andy said.

"Open the door!" Hookie-the-Goblin cried as he banged his heels against the candy door.

"You run home before the Snitznoodle returns!" Mrs. Cookie called.

"Ha, ha, ha!" Hookie yelled. "I guess you think I don't know where the Snitznoodle has gone. He has gone home for his nightie. That's what! And he won't come back until he finds it. And he won't find it because I have it right here." And the goblin laughed so hard he rolled upon the sugar ground. "Ha, ha, ha! So the Snitznoodle will never come back."

"You are a mean, unkind goblin!" Raggedy Ann said. "How would you feel if someone should take your nightie? You wouldn't like that, would you?"

"I have my nightie with me," the goblin said. "I've come to live with the nice cookie people!"

"We don't want you to live with us," Mrs. Cookie told him. "The first thing you would do would be to nibble us!"

"I *am* very hungry," the goblin said. "Unless you open the door and let me in, I shall start nibbling the door, for I see it is made of cake and covered with candy icing." And in a few moments, Hookie-the-Goblin had nibbled a large hole in the nice cookie people's front door.

Maybe it tasted good, but no one but a mean goblin would think of nibbling a person's front door.

Raggedy Ann knew that if Hookie got into the house, he would surely nibble one of the Cookie people, and Mrs. Cookie thought so, too, for she said:

"I wish the Snitznoodle would hurry back."

"He won't be back!" Hookie-the-Goblin declared. By this time Hookie had nibbled a hole large enough to put his head through.

"What is that you have on the table?" Hookie asked. "It looks like something to eat," It was something to eat. It was a large plate of cream puffs which Mrs. Cookie had just taken from the oven. But no one answered Hookie because he had been very rude and nibbled the front door and put his head through the hole.

Raggedy Ann whispered to Raggedy Andy and Little Weakie. Immediately Raggedy Andy and Little Weakie caught Hookie by the ears, so that the goblin could not get his head back through the hole.

Then, while Raggedy Andy and Little Weakie held the goblin, Raggedy Ann got Mrs. Cookie's largest pancake paddle and ran out the back door.

"Don't let him go!" Raggedy Ann called in.

"We won't," Raggedy Andy replied. And they didn't either.

My! How Hookie-the-Goblin howled when Raggedy Ann paddy-whacked him with the large pancake paddle. Hookie wiggled and twisted and kicked, but Raggedy Andy and Little Weakie held his ears so tightly, the goblin could not escape.

"Now! I expect that will be enough," Raggedy Ann called as she gave Hookie just one more hard smack.

So Raggedy Andy and Little Weakie let go of the goblin's ears and he pulled his head out of the cookie door.

"You'll be sorry!" Hookie howled as he wiped his large eyes. Then seeing Raggedy Ann standing behind him with the pancake paddle, Hookie grabbed her and started running home. But just as he turned the corner of the house, the Snitznoodle arrived and bumped him over. And, before the goblin could get to his feet, the Snitznoodle had given him three hard thumps which sent him rolling head over heels again.

The kind Snitznoodle helped Raggedy Ann to her feet and brushed the brown sugar ground from her apron.

"I just came back to tell the nice cookie people that I can't live with them because some one has taken my nightie."

"It was the goblin," Raggedy Ann said. "And here is your nightie right on the front doorstep. Hookie tried to make us think it was his own nightie for he wanted to live with the nice cookie people, too!"

"I am so glad we found it," the Snitznoodle said as he picked up his nightie, "for now I can live with the cookie people and thump the goblin whenever he comes around.

CHAPTER SIX

A QUEER SNOWSTORM

*T*HE Snitznoodle hung his nightie behind the bedroom door. The cookie people were very glad the Snitznoodle had returned to live with them, for he was such a nice, kindly creature.

Now that the Snitznoodle had come to live with the nice cookie people, it made things a lot easier for Mrs. Cookie. Not that she had too much to do. No, not that. But when Mrs. Cookie baked a lovely cake chicken and stuffed it with chopped nuts and pineapple and everything nice, she never had to throw any of it out, for the Snitznoodle was sure to eat all that was left. And besides, the Snitznoodle always *did* the dishes.

The way the Snitznoodle *did* the dishes was to take them out in the yard and eat them. This was a lot easier than washing them. The dishes were made of thin dough like Nabiscos and covered with icing to make them shiny like real-for-sure dishes. Anyone could eat that sort of dish, and enjoy it, too.

It was after dinner. The Snitznoodle had taken the

dishes out in the front yard to eat them; and he was having a very pleasant time doing it. The cookie man had gone out to the back yard to give the cookie cow and the cookie pigs six buckets of granulated sugar for their dinner. And Raggedy Ann was pretending to play the cookie organ in the living room. So no one heard the nice cookie man cry out when Hookie-the-Goblin came up in back of him and captured him. No one heard him cry except the cookie cow.

"Now I have you, Mr. Cookie!" the goblin cried as he stuffed Mr. Cookie in a large paper bag and tied a string around the top.

"My, won't the cookie man taste good?" Hookie-the-Goblin said to himself as he tossed the paper bag over his shoulder. "The cookie man is made of nice chocolate cookie and his clothes are covered with candy icing. I shall nibble him and nibble him until I am not the least bit hungry."

And the goblin walked towards his home.

Poor, nice Mr. Cookie did not like being tied up in a paper bag, and he knew very well that the goblin would eat him when he reached home.

"I wish Raggedy Andy and Little Weakie would rescue me," the cookie man thought. "But they will never know what has become of me."

After Hookie-the-Goblin had walked a long way with his heavy load, he grew tired. "I guess I'll sit down and rest a bit," he said.

He had been sitting but a moment when he hopped to his feet crying, "Dear me! I must hurry and get the cookie man home! A great black cloud is coming and I am sure it is going to rain. And if it rains, the cookie man will get all wet and soggy, and won't be a bit nice to eat." So Hookie lifted the bag to his back again and started on. Pretty soon he began slipping this way and that and finally down he fell.

"I wonder what can be the trouble?" Hookie asked himself. The trouble was that it was powdered sugar snow—

not rain—that had fallen from the black cloud and lay three inches thick on that part of the road. And there the goblin had to lie, unable to get up.

Meanwhile Raggedy Ann had grown tired of pretending to play upon the cookie organ. She asked, "Where are Mr. Cookie and the Snitznoodle? Where can they be?"

"The Snitznoodle is out in the front yard *doing* the dishes," Mrs. Cookie said. "And Mr. Cookie is out back giving the cookie cow and pigs their granulated sugar feed."

Raggedy Ann looked out of the window and said, "Look! It's beginning to snow."

"So it is!" Mrs. Cookie laughed.

"Whee!" Raggedy Andy ran outside and scooped up a handful of the snow. "It isn't cold snow at all."

"Oh, no," Mrs. Cookie replied. "It isn't real snow you know, it is powdered sugar snow!" Every one went out in the yard to see it snow powdered sugar. The Raggedys had never seen snow like this before.

"You must put on paper hats," Mrs. Cookie said. "Powdered sugar snow will get into your yarn hair and make it sticky. We never go out in the snow for very long at a time," she continued, "for cookie people get wet and sticky when the snow melts. That is why I do not like Mr. Cookie to be out in this kind of weather. If he gets wet, he has cookie rheumatism, and I have to put him in the oven and bake him until he gets dry. I can't imagine what can be keeping him!"

Mrs. Cookie called as loudly as she could; the cookie man did not answer. But the Snitznoodle came running up, for he had finished eating the last cookie dish.

"Dear me!" he said. "The cookie dishes were nice with the powdered sugar snow on them. Where is Mr. Cookie?"

No one could answer, so they all went down to where the cookie cow was eating the bucket of granulated sugar. "Where is Mr. Cookie?" Raggedy Ann asked the cow.

"Hookie-the-Goblin came and put him in a large paper bag and carried him away," the cow replied. (The cookie cow could talk as well as the cookie people for they were all made of magical dough.)

It had stopped snowing by this time, so the Snitznoodle and Raggedy Andy started to look for the goblin. Presently they came to where they could see the goblin's tracks in the powdered sugar snow and they noticed that he had stopped to rest every once in a while.

"We'll soon catch up with him," the Snitznoodle said as he lifted Raggedy Andy to his back. "I can run very fast, so I'll carry you." The Snitznoodle ran very fast and before long they saw a strange object coming towards them. The Snitznoodle thought it was a Hikagee. He and Raggedy hid behind a tree until the Hikagee drew close. Then Raggedy Andy gave a *whoop!* and threw his hat in the air. "It's the cookie man inside the paper bag!" he cried. And, indeed, it was! The cookie man had punched his feet through two holes in the bottom of the bag and was walking home. He could not get out of the bag because the goblin had tied a string at the top.

Raggedy Andy soon cut the string, and he and the Snitz-noodle helped the cookie man out.

"Mercy!" he said. "I have had a great adventure, and as soon as we get home I'll tell you all about it."

They were glad to see Mr. Cookie safe and sound.

"I never thought I should get back home again!" the cookie man exclaimed when he had had a dish of ice cream to rest him. "But you should see old Mr. Hookie-the-Goblin!" Mr. Cookie laughed. "I could peep through a little hole in the paper bag and watch him. He carried me for a while and then got tired, and sat down to rest. Well, sir,

the powdered sugar snow fell on him and melted, and he was as sticky as a wet lollypop. I left him sitting on the ground, and he was covered with the powdered sugar snow. In the beginning, when the snow melted on Hookie and ran down to the ground, it made him so tired he fell down. He must have gone to sleep for a while, for when he tried to get to his feet, he was snowed under. All this while I was wiggling my feet until I had punched two holes in the paper bag. Now I could walk. I stepped around in front of Hookie and cried in a loud voice, 'Ahaa! Mr. Hookie, I am Whangdoodle and I have come to gobble you up! Shall I begin with your nose, or shall I begin with your toes?'"

"My! How that goblin twisted and wiggled to get away!" Mr. Cookie laughed. "But he was stuck fast, so I said, 'Ah! Mr. Goblin, you may wiggle and you may twiggle, but you shall never escape from the Whangdoodle. Now I am going home to get my knife and fork; when I come back I will eat you up completely!' And I walked away chuckling to myself, for I knew that Hookie felt the same about being nibbled as I did."

"You did just right!" Raggedy Andy laughed. "Perhaps now the goblin will know how we felt, and will not try to nibble any one again."

"That was the only reason I fooled him," Mr. Cookie said. "Perhaps it isn't right to frighten a person, but let's hope this time we have taught the goblin a lesson. The thought of the Whangdoodle returning to eat him will not be a pleasant recollection for Hookie!"

"Well, if I had been there, I should have given Hookie a couple of hard thumps," the Snitznoodle said, as he passed the jelly tarts that Mrs. Cookie had just finished baking.

And so these good friends sat and laughed and talked, and they soon forgot all about Hookie and his meanness, for how can people think of disagreeable things if their minds are filled with friendliness, and their mouths with nice fresh jelly tarts?

CHAPTER SEVEN

WHERE IS THE SNITZNOODLE?

RAGGEDY ANDY was gazing out the window. "Look!" he cried as he ran to the door. "Hookie-the-Goblin has taken all the cookie chickens and ducks. I just saw him put the last one into a bag!"

"I shall catch him and give him another thump!" the Snitznoodle cried as he ran out the door. Hookie-the-Goblin saw the Snitznoodle, so he threw the bag over his shoulder and ran, lickety-split, as fast as he could run. And the kind Snitznoodle ran after Hookie, lickety-split, too. But though the Snitznoodle could run fast, the goblin could run faster Over logs and bushes the two raced until the goblin came to a queer house. Into this the goblin ran, and banged the door behind him.

The Snitznoodle had never seen such a house before. There was one room downstairs and three rooms, one above the other, on top of the first room.

The Snitznoodle ran to the door and thumped upon it as hard as he could.

"Who is it?" the goblin asked.

"It's me!" the Snitznoodle replied. "And I want you to open the door."

"Ha, ha! I knew it was you all the time," the goblin laughed. "But I just wanted to see if you would pretend you were someone else!"

If you do not open the door, I shall thump it so hard it will break in two!" the Snitznoodle cried.

"Aha, Mr. Snitznoodle! You can thump all you please, for the door is iron and I'd like to see any Snitznoodle break it in two!"

"Then I shall wait out here for you to come out, and when you do, you'd better expect a few hard thumps."

"I sha'n't come out," the goblin replied. And the Snitznoodle could hear him going up the stairs.

"I have enough cookie chickens and ducks to last me a long time," the goblin said to himself, "so the Snitznoodle will get hungry long before I do, then he will have to return to the cookie people and I can walk out without getting a single hard thump."

But Hookie-the-Goblin did not know that before the Snitznoodle went to live with the cookie people he had never eaten anything except wind sandwiches. So, when the Snitznoodle got hungry, he just took out his knife and made himself fifteen wind sandwiches and piled them beside him upon the steps. Then he had a very nice dinner and wasn't even a little bit hungry.

The goblin could not see the wind sandwiches, so he laughed to himself. "Ha, the Snitznoodle will soon be getting hungry." But the Snitznoodle didn't get hungry. He just sat there and waited.

When it grew dark and the nice, kind Snitznoodle did not return to the cookie house, Raggedy Ann said, "I wonder what has become of the Snitznoodle? Do you suppose he followed Hookie clear to his home in the grotto?"

No one could answer because no one knew.

"Maybe the Snitznoodle has caught the goblin and is still thumping him," the cookie man said.

"Perhaps!" Raggedy Andy replied. "But still I do not believe the Snitznoodle would thump the goblin steadily for two hours."

Raggedy Ann did not wish to go to bed until the Snitznoodle returned. But after a while, when it grew very late (fifteen minutes of nine by the candy covered cuckoo clock) Raggedy Ann and the others all went to sleep. And while they all slept soundly in their beds, the brave Snitznoodle leaned back against the door sill of the queer little house and went to sleep, too.

"I shall give him a surprise," the goblin giggled as he slowly let a rope down over the Snitznoodle.

As soon as the rope was around the Snitznoodle, Hookie-the-Goblin pulled him into the room at the top of the house.

No one except Hookie knows how long the Snitznoodle slept. When he finally awakened, the Snitznoodle found himself sitting in a chair, tied hand and foot, so that he could not get away.

"Oh, you can wiggle and twiggle all you wish," Hookie laughed. "I have tied you with goblin knots and only goblins know how to untie them."

The next morning when Raggedy Ann and her friends came to the breakfast table, Mr. Cookie asked, "Didn't the Snitznoodle come home last night?"

"No," Raggedy Ann replied. "I am afraid something must have happened to the nice, kind Snitznoodle."

"I shall take the cookie puppydog and follow the Snitznoodle," Raggedy Andy said.

So Raggedy Andy called the little cookie puppydog and they followed the Snitznoodle's trail until they came to the queer little house.

The cookie puppydog whined and jumped about the door.

"What do you want down there?" Hookie-the-Goblin howled as he poked his head out of an upstairs window.

"We want the Snitznoodle," Raggedy Andy replied.

"The Snitznoodle isn't here," the goblin told him.

"Oh, what a big fib!" Raggedy Andy called back. "He *is* here and you know it, Mr. Hookie-the-Goblin!"

"Well, then, I'll tell you, Raggedy Andy," Hookie laughed. "I have captured the Snitznoodle and have him tied to a chair, and just as soon as I can borrow a sausage grinder I shall make sausage out of the Snitznoodle."

"What a mean thing to do to a nice, kind Snitznoodle," Raggedy Andy said to himself as he and the cookie puppydog walked sadly back to the cookie house and told their friends the sorrowful story.

"We must rescue the Snitznoodle!" Raggedy Ann said.

"But how?" Raggedy Andy asked. "The goblin has the Snitznoodle tied to a chair and the doors are bolted."

"We must all sit down and think ever and ever so hard," Raggedy Ann said. "There must be some way to rescue our good friend."

Mrs. Cookie brought out a large plate of cream puffs and lady fingers with jelly on them and a large dish of ice cream apiece, for she knew they would all be able to think better if they had something nice to eat.

When Little Weakie had eaten six cream puffs, nine lady fingers and two more plates of ice cream he cried, "Aha! I have thought of a way to rescue the Snitznoodle."

"Then hurry and tell us, Little Weakie!" Raggedy Ann said. "I have ripped two stitches from the back of my head trying to think."

"It will be as easy as pie!" Little Weakie laughed. "You can bake a cookie balloon, Raggedy Ann. And we can take it to Hookie's house and I will get in the balloon and sail up to the roof. Then I will jump from the balloon and climb down the chimney and rescue the Snitznoodle."

"That sounds like a very good idea, Little Weakie!" Raggedy Ann said. "I will bake the balloon out of cream puff dough so that it will be light and fluffy and sail through the air."

Raggedy Ann asked them all to help her so that the balloon would be made quickly. So they rolled up their sleeves and helped. Then, when they found the oven too small for a large balloon, Raggedy Ann made a lot of small ones.

When the balloons were baked they were so light they sailed out of the oven door as soon as it was opened. It was fun to chase them about the room and catch them.

When all the balloons were tied together, Raggedy Ann and Raggedy Andy and Little Weakie and the cookie people took them down to the strange tall house of Hookie-the-Goblin.

Little Weakie held on to the rope and sailed up over the roof of Hookie's house. He jumped to the roof and the balloons sailed away out of sight.

"Now I shall climb down the chimney and rescue the nice, kind Snitznoodle," Little Weakie called down from the roof.

But as he said this, the window at the top of the house opened and Hookie-the-Goblin poked his head out.

"What did you say?" he asked Raggedy Ann.

"I didn't say anything," Raggedy Ann answered.

"Then who did?" the goblin asked. "I heard some one say something about rescuing the Snitznoodle."

"It was I who said it," Little Weakie replied looking over the roof at the goblin. "I shall rescue the nice, kind Snitznoodle because it isn't any fun being captured by a mean goblin and tied to a chair."

"Ha, ha, ha,!" the goblin laughed very rudely. "What I wish to know is this: How do you expect to rescue the Snitznoodle when you are on the roof?"

"That will be easy," Little Weakie replied. "I shall climb down the chimney and wrestle you ever so hard. Then you will be glad to untie the Snitznoodle and let him escape."

At this Hookie-the-Goblin laughed so loudly, he rolled from the window back into the room, and it was a long time before he could stop laughing long enough to come to the window again. When he did, he said, "You have thought of everything except one thing, Little Weakie."

"And what is that, I'd like to know?" Little Weakie asked.

"Why," Hookie howled with glee, "there isn't any chimney for you to climb down. That's what!" And when Little Weakie looked about the roof, sure enough, there was no chimney at all. And there he was, high up on top of the goblin's house with no way of getting down.

Raggedy Ann and Raggedy Andy and the cookie people felt very sad and Little Weakie felt as sad as the rest, for the roof was much too high for him to jump to the ground.

My, how the mean little goblin made fun of them all!

He even stuck out his tongue at them, which was a very rude thing to do even for a goblin, and goodness knows they are rude enough at times.

"Now, Little Weakie will have to be rescued as well as the Snitznoodle. And if you are not careful, perhaps I shall capture all of you before I am through. And if I do," the goblin chuckled, "I shall eat every one of the cookie people, candy shoes and hats and all."

"You are afraid to come down here!" Raggedy Andy said. "I would wrestle with you if you did."

"Pooh! I'm not afraid," the goblin howled. "But it would be foolish if I did come down there just to wrestle with you. You will have to find a way to come up here if you wish to wrestle with me, Raggedy Andy. But you can never find a way to get inside my house, so you will never rescue the Snitznoodle!"

"You will be sorry for the way you are acting," Raggedy Ann said.

Hookie laughed again and banged the window shut.

"Let's go away where we can talk without the goblin over-hearing us," Raggedy Ann said. "I am certain we shall find a way to rescue both the Snitznoodle and Little Weakie."

So the Raggedys and the cookie people went into the woods a ways, and sat down so they might talk things over without the goblin hearing.

The Raggedys and the cookie people were very quiet, for one has to be quiet when one is trying to think hard.

That is one reason why some children can not study properly, they wiggle and twist about too much.

Finally Raggedy Ann said, "I have thought of a way in which we may rescue the Snitznoodle. Later we may think of a way to rescue Little Weakie!"

"What is it, Raggedy Ann?" they all wanted to know.

"Well," Raggedy Ann questioned, "do you remember how little Snow White's stepmother fooled little Snow White?"

The cookie people had never heard the story, so Raggedy Ann told it to them. "And," Raggedy Ann ended, "little Snow White's stepmother, the mean old queen, disguised herself as an old woman and came to the house where Snow White lived with the seven cunning little dwarfs." When Raggedy Ann had finished the rest of the story of little Snow White, she said, "I believe that if I disguise myself, I can go to Hookie's door pretending to sell something. And when I get inside, I can rescue the Snitznoodle."

"Whee!" everyone cried. "Raggedy Ann is right. It will be easy to fool old Hookie-the-Goblin. And, when he opens the door, we can all rush in and help Raggedy Ann rescue the Snitznoodle."

So Raggedy Ann and her friends walked away from Hookie's house and when Hookie saw them going he laughed to himself, "Ha, ha, ha!" just like that, only of course a great deal louder. "Now they will not bother me again!"

CHAPTER EIGHT

THE THUMPS ON THE DOOR

IN THE cookie house, Raggedy Ann disguised herself as a witch, and with a little basket of goodies on her arm, she returned to the home of the goblin. In her basket were eleven cookies with white icing, six cream puffs and nine jelly tarts. Goblins are quite fond of these, and no wonder for they are very, very good.

When Raggedy Andy and the cookie people were safely hidden in the woods near the goblin's house, Raggedy Ann disguised as the witch came walking down the path crying, "Nice fresh cream puffs! Nice fresh jelly tarts! Nice fresh cookies with white candy icing! Who wishes to buy? Who wishes to try?"

Hookie-the-Goblin was upstairs teasing the Snitznoodle.

"Listen!" Hookie-the-Goblin said.

"I haven't made any noise," the Snitznoodle replied.

"I know it," the goblin cried. "But you might say something and I wish to hear what that person is crying."

"I did not intend saying anything," the Snitznoodle said. "So you may listen all you wish!"

"Will you please be still?" the goblin howled.

"Yes, I will!" the Snitznoodle said.

Of course the goblin could not hear what Raggedy Ann was crying when he and the Snitznoodle were talking, so he went downstairs and opened a crack in the door.

"What are you saying, Mrs. Witch?" he asked.

"I am selling cream puffs, jelly tarts and nice cookies with candy icing!" Raggedy Ann replied. Hookie-the-Goblin suddenly opened the door and pulled Raggedy Ann inside with one jerk; then he slammed and locked the door before Raggedy Andy or the cookie people saw what had happened.

Soon Hookie-the-Goblin poked his head from the upstairs window and laughed, "Ha, ha! You thought you could fool me, didn't you? Why! I knew it was Raggedy Ann by her shoe button eyes. Now I have captured the Snitznoodle, Little Weakie and Raggedy Ann." Then he slammed the window with a bang and left Raggedy Andy and the cookie people feeling sadder and sadder and sadder every minute.

"How shall we ever rescue our dear friends?" Raggedy Andy asked.

"Let's see," the cookie man said. "The goblin wishes to make the Snitznoodle into sausage, doesn't he? Well then, Raggedy Andy must take a sausage grinder to the goblin's door, and when the goblin reaches out for the grinder, Raggedy Andy can wrestle him."

"That is a good idea," Raggedy Andy decided. "We shall borrow Mrs. Cookie's sausage grinder."

"But I have none!" Mrs. Cookie replied. "We cookie people never eat anything except cream puffs and things like that, so we have no use for sausage grinders. In fact, I do not know what a sausage grinder looks like."

"It is a thing like a hand organ," Raggedy Andy told her, "except it does not have a music box at the other end of the handle. It has a place to put the things to be ground up into sausage. Then you turn the handle 'round and 'round just as if you were playing a grind-organ, and sausage comes out instead of music."

"Oh!" Mrs. Cookie cried as she ran into the cookie house and came running out again, "do you mean something like this? This is a food chopper and I use it to grind up the nuts and raisins and fruit I put into the cakes and cookies."

"Whee!" Raggedy Andy cried. "That is just what we need! I'll bet two silver nickels that I shall rescue our friends. You wait here and I will be back in a few minutes."

Raggedy Andy hurried to the goblin's house with the food chopper under his arm. Raggedy Andy thumped upon the goblin's door with the food chopper, *thump, thump!*

"Who is it?" the goblin asked as he poked his head out of the window at the top of the house.

"It's Raggedy Andy, and I have brought you a food chopper to make sausage with. Mrs. Cookie will lend it to you."

"Then I will come right down and get it," Hookie-the-Goblin said, closing the window.

Raggedy Andy heard the goblin running down stairs, *clippety, clippety,* his footsteps coming nearer all the time. Then Raggedy Andy heard Hookie unlocking the iron door. The key went *click, clock,* and the door was unlocked and opened a teeny-weeny crack; one eye of the goblin peered out. Raggedy Andy held the food chopper behind him.

"Are you trying to fool me, Raggedy Andy?" the goblin asked. "I do not see any sausage grinder."

"That is because you are only looking with one eye, Mr. Hookie!" Raggedy Andy replied. So the goblin opened the door a little more so that his long nose stuck out.

Quick as a wink, Raggedy Andy pushed the sausage grinder upon the goblin's long nose and gave the handle a twist.

"*Wow!*" the goblin howled as he kicked the door open and sat down hard upon the doorstep.

Raggedy Andy let go of the sausage grinder and said,

73

"Don't try to pull it off, Mr. Hookie, or you will lose your long nose." Then he rushed inside to where Raggedy Ann was locked in a closet.

It took only a moment for Raggedy Andy to unlock the closet door, and then he and Raggedy Ann ran upstairs and cut the ropes which fastened the nice, kind Snitznoodle.

When they got back, Hookie-the-Goblin was still sitting on the front steps with the sausage grinder hanging from his nose. Raggedy Ann gently unfastened the sausage grinder from Hookie's nose, for she had a candy heart and did not like to see any one hurt.

"Anyway," the goblin cried as he ran into his house, "Little Weakie is still up on the roof!"

"Yoo-hoo!" Little Weakie shouted to his friends below.

"We shall try to rescue you," the Snitznoodle called back.

"You'd better run away as fast as you can!" Hookie-the-Goblin cried from his high window. "I expect the Hungry Howloon here any minute, and he will capture you as soon as he comes."

"Who is afraid of a Hungry Howloon?" the Snitznoodle cried. "Not I, I am sure. I shall climb right up the water spout to the roof and help Little Weakie down."

So the Snitznoodle climbed the water spout and rescued Little Weakie.

"Let's run back to the cookie house," said Raggedy Ann.

Mrs. Cookie had a nice dinner waiting for them. She had made a large cake turkey with chopped raisin dressing and chocolate gravy. And for pretend-tea, they had pink lemonade and red soda pop. It was a very nice dinner with the ice cream afterwards and they all enjoyed it.

After dinner, Mrs. Cookie gave each one an extra large all-day-sucker lollypop. And while they were enjoying the lollypops there came a loud *bang, bang, bang!* upon the door. The little cake house shook so hard that large pieces of icing fell from the roof.

"It sounds like a giant!" Little Weakie declared.

"If it isn't, it is surely a very rude person who thumps so hard," Raggedy Ann said. "If I were you I wouldn't go to the door, Mrs. Cookie."

"It is probably an agent!" Raggedy Andy declared. "They always knock loudly, as if they were in a great hurry. But when you go to the door, you can hardly get rid of them."

BANG! BANG! BANG! Again came the loud thumps upon the candy door and a great piece of the candy ceiling fell clattering to the floor.

"It's a strange looking creature!" Raggedy Andy said as he peeped from the window.

"Who is knocking so rudely upon my candy door?" Mrs. Cookie asked.

"The Hungry Howloon!" a voice replied.

"Then you may run right home to your mama," Mrs. Cookie said.

"But I haven't any mama!" the Hungry Howloon replied in a loud voice. "And, besides, I am very hungry and I want you to open the door so that I can eat every one of the cookie people."

"But you must not eat the cookie people, Mr. Howloon!" Raggedy Ann said.

"Hookie-the-Goblin said that I could," the Hungry Howloon answered. "He said they were made of chocolate and covered with candy icing!"

"They are," Raggedy Ann said, "but they do not wish to be eaten."

"Then will someone please tell me what I am to do?"

75

the Hungry Howloon asked. "The longer I stand here, the hungrier and hungrier I become."

"Why don't you run back to the goblin's house and ask him to give you something to eat?" Raggedy Andy asked.

"I never thought of that," the Hungry Howloon replied.

"Mercy! I'm glad he has gone," Mr. Cookie sighed. "I always feel cold crumbs creep up my back when anyone speaks of eating me."

"We shall not let anyone eat you," the nice, kind Snitznoodle promised.

"Just the same," Mrs. Cookie said, "I hope the Hungry Howloon does not return."

"I do not believe the Hungry Howloon will return," the Snitznoodle said, wishing to make the cookie people feel happier.

"No! I am sure he will not return," Little Weakie said.

But both he and the Snitznoodle were mistaken. In a short time here came the Hungry Howloon galloping back to the cookie house. *BANG! BANG! THUMP! THUMP!* he hammered upon the door.

"What shall we do?" the cookie people asked.

"There is nothing we can do!" Raggedy Ann replied.

The Hungry Howloon waited a few moments, then he began thumping on the door again. The candy dishes rattled and clattered to the floor and the whole house shook.

"Mercy! He will break in the door!" Mrs. Cookie cried.

And soon that is just what happened. The Hungry Howloon broke the candy covered cookie door right off its candy hinges and came walking into the cookie house.

The Hungry Howloon had never seen Raggedy Ann nor Raggedy Andy, nor any of the others, so he did not recognize the difference between them and the cookie people.

"Show me which ones are good to eat so that I can begin eating," he cried. "I am getting hungrier every minute."

As no one answered, the Hungry Howloon caught Raggedy Andy and said, "I shall start eating this one."

Raggedy Andy knew it wouldn't hurt him even if the Howloon did eat him, for he was made of cloth and stuffed with nice soft, white cotton. So Raggedy Andy just smiled his painted smile and did not say a word.

Mrs. Cookie, though, did not wish to see Raggedy Andy eaten, so she said, "That is Raggedy Andy. You must not eat him. I am Mrs. Cookie."

The Hungry Howloon let go of Raggedy Andy and caught hold of Mrs. Cookie. "Then I shall eat you!"

The kind Snitznoodle and Little Weakie held their breaths.

The Hungry Howloon turned Mrs. Cookie over and over. "Which is the proper way to eat cookie people?" he asked. "Shall I begin at the feet or at the head?"

"I shouldn't begin at all, if I were you," Raggedy Ann said.

"But I am so awful, very, terribliest terrible hungry!" the Howloon cried. "And each moment I get hungrier. Please tell me which way to begin, for I wish to have nice table manners."

"I suppose I shall have to wrestle the Hungry Howloon," Raggedy Andy decided, "for I shall not let him eat Mrs. Cookie."

"Yes," the kind Snitznoodle said, "you wrestle him first, Raggedy Andy. Then if you can not wrestle him hard enough, I will give him a hard thump."

"Ha, ha! So you wish to wrestle, do you, Raggedy Andy?" the Hungry Howloon cried as he put Mrs. Cookie down in a chair. "Then I shall wrestle with you. But I warn you that the more I wrestle, the hungrier I become, and I howl very loudly all the time I wrestle."

"Ha!" Raggedy Andy cried as he rolled up his sleeves. "Howl all you wish, we shall not mind!"

"Wait a minute," the Hungry Howloon cried. "It isn't fair to roll up your sleeves when I haven't any sleeves to roll up. I sha'n't wrestle you."

"All right," Raggedy Andy agreed. "Then I won't roll up my sleeves. My! But you would have been wrestled hard if I could just roll up my sleeves." Raggedy Andy rolled his sleeves down again.

"One, two, three," the Snitznoodle cried, and Raggedy Andy and the Hungry Howloon rushed at each other. It sounded as if Raggedy Andy had struck a bass drum when he hit the Howloon and before his friends knew what had happened Raggedy Andy had picked up the Hungry Howloon and had thrown him across the room. The Hungry Howloon hit a sharp corner of the candy fireplace.

The Hungry Howloon stood still with a queer expression upon his face as if he felt very sad and greatly surprised at the same time.

Then everyone heard a tiny whistling sound and the Hungry Howloon's legs began to sag beneath him. No one said a word while the Hungry Howloon shrank and wrinkled until he fell to the floor a wrinkled heap.

"Why," Raggedy Ann cried in surprise, "the Hungry Howloon is only made of thin rubber. When he struck the sharp corner of the fireplace he was punctured. Poor thing! No wonder he has always been hungry. He was as empty as a football.

And Raggedy Ann felt so sorry for the Hungry Howloon, she picked him up and draped him over a candy covered cookie chair. "There's the puncture!" she said. "Let us fix it and pump him up again. Why look!" she cried as she held up the Howloon's head, "he has no mouth at all, so he could not have eaten the cookie people if he had tried. We have all had a fright for nothing!" And Raggedy Ann laughed.

"Isn't that always the way?" she asked.

CHAPTER NINE

AN UPSETTING TIME

"WHY wouldn't it be a good idea to stuff the Hungry Howloon with cake chickens and cream puffs and cookies?" Raggedy Ann demanded. "Then he would never be hungry because he would never be empty."

Mrs. Cookie brought six cake chickens and a lot of cream puffs and cookies and Raggedy Ann snipped a hole in the Hungry Howloon's rubber sides and put the goodies in. Then she put in a lot of lollypops, for they are nice, you know. But she took the sticks off first so that they would not punch through the Howloon's sides. Then Raggedy Ann patched the holes with sticky molasses and when it was dry Raggedy Andy and the Snitznoodle took turns pumping up the Hungry Howloon.

When the Hungry Howloon stood up, as nice and as round as he had been before, he laughed and said, "I don't feel hungry now, so I shall not eat any of you." And Mrs. Cookie felt so happy, she gave the Hungry Howloon a hug and told him that he could live at the cookie house and be a free boarder just like the Snitznoodle.

"Thank you, Mrs. Cookie," the Howloon said. "It wasn't

any fun being as empty as a toy balloon. Now I shall never be a Hungry Howloon again. I shall be only a Howloon, and that makes me happy!"

And of course that made the others happy, too, for happiness is just like a ray of sunshine coming through a crack into a dark room; it lights up everything around it. And so the Howloon's happiness made the others happy.

"I believe I shall take a little walk," the Howloon said. "I am stuffed so full, I feel drowsy."

Raggedy Ann laughed. "Whenever anyone has too much to eat, he feels drowsy, so he should either take a nice nap, or else run out in the fresh air and play."

"I shall go out in the cookie garden and play, then," the Howloon decided.

Raggedy Ann and her friends watched the Howloon as he walked into the garden, and they were all very glad that he had turned out to be a friend.

"I can tell you," Raggedy Ann said with a smile. "A good friend is like a beautiful flower. And each new friend you add to your list means another flower added to your friendship garden. And if you will tend them with the spirit of kindness, and warm them with the sunshine of love, you will soon have a lovely garden which will bloom forever."

And so Raggedy Ann and her friends laughed and talked, and the Howloon, very contented now, visited the cookie cow and the cookie pigs out in the cookie barnyard. He had so many pleasant thoughts in his Howloon head that he did not hear Hookie-the-Goblin slip up quietly behind him. He was surprised to feel a rope fall over his head, and to hear the goblin cry, "*Aha!*"

Then the goblin ran towards his home, pulling the Howloon behind him. "I listened at the cookie house," Hookie laughed back over his shoulder. "And I know just what happened there."

The poor Howloon could not answer, because the rope

was too tight around his rubber neck; he could only bounce along in back of the goblin. And he hit against the trees and candy stones as he bounced along.

This did not hurt the Howloon a bit, since he was made of rubber, but he did not enjoy it very much. And each time the Howloon hit a tree with a *blump*, the goblin laughed. That shows just how unpleasant a goblin can be when he wishes to be mean.

"Where do you suppose the Howloon is now?" wondered Raggedy Ann when Mrs. Cookie placed a lot of good things to eat upon the table. "He has been away a long time. Maybe he has gone to sleep out in the garden. I will run out and see!"

Raggedy Ann went into the garden, and called, and called, but the Howloon did not answer. Then the others, joining Raggedy Ann, came to the place where the goblin had thrown the rope over the Howloon's head and they could see plainly where the Howloon had been dragged along.

"I'll bet a nickel that Hookie-the-Goblin has captured him, too," Little Weakie said.

"Raggedy Andy and I had better run to the goblin's house and see," the Snitznoodle decided. "So he and Raggedy Andy ran until they came to Hookie's front door. Then Raggedy Andy took a stone and tapped upon the door. Hookie put his head out of his window and said, "Stop knocking upon my iron door with a stone, Raggedy Andy, for I shall not let you in."

"Did you capture the Howloon?" Raggedy Andy asked.

"Aha! Indeed, I did!" the goblin replied. "And I shall keep him a prisoner, too, because I know you filled him with cream puffs and other good things."

"If you take the nice things out of the Howloon you will be sorry," the Snitznoodle shouted. But Hookie only laughed and banged his window shut.

"Isn't he just the meanest goblin you ever saw?" the Snitznoodle asked Raggedy Andy, as the two sat upon the goblin's step and tried to think of a way to rescue their friend, the Howloon.

As the two friends sat there, the Snitznoodle put his hand in his pocket and pulled out a little bean. "It used to be a jumping bean," he told Raggedy Andy. "But now it doesn't jump any more. Not even a smidgin!"

So he tossed the bean upon the ground and it rolled under some leaves. The Snitznoodle did not know that the little bean was a magical bean. Neither did Raggedy Andy.

But the little magical bean started growing right away, and the two sat and watched the bean vine climb right up the side of Hookie's house.

"Ha!" Raggedy Andy cried. "That bean must have been a cousin to the magic bean which Jack-of-the-Beanstalk planted, and which grew up to the giant's land." When the bean stalk reached the goblin's window the Snitznoodle and Raggedy Andy climbed up. And, they had just reached the height of the window when the goblin ran out the door and whacked the bean stalk with a hatchet. Raggedy Andy and the Snitznoodle tumbled to the ground and the goblin ran into the house and locked the door behind him.

"That was the time I fooled you—just as Jack fooled the giant," Hookie laughed.

"Anyway," the Snitznoodle and Raggedy Andy called back, "it didn't hurt us a bit!"

Raggedy Ann was sitting in a white candy covered rocking chair in Mrs. Cookie's house. "I believe it is about time Raggedy Andy and the nice, kind Snitznoodle were returning from the Goblin's house," she said.

"I hope the goblin has not captured them as well as the Howloon," answered Mr. Cookie.

"We'll wait a few minutes and then if they do not return, we shall walk down there and see what has happened," Raggedy Ann said.

So they sat and waited and rocked until the candy cuckoo clock had ticked five candy minutes; then as Raggedy Andy had not returned, Raggedy Ann and the Cookie people walked down to Hookie's house.

When they reached there, Raggedy Ann took a stone and knocked upon the iron door. No one answered. So Raggedy Ann knocked again.

Still no one answered. "I believe Hookie is not at home!" Mrs. Cookie said. "If he were he would have put his head out of the window by now."

"What shall we do?" Raggedy Ann asked.

Before anyone could reply a stone went whizzing above Raggedy Ann's head and broke into pieces upon the iron door. And then Hookie called to them, "Hey! Go away from my house! I am not at home!"

Raggedy Ann and her friends ran away from Hookie's house as fast as they could. "You'd better run!" the goblin cried. "If you are not careful I shall capture you just as I have captured the Hungry Howloon, Raggedy Andy and the Snitznoodle."

"Oh, Hookie! You mean creature!" Raggedy Ann called back at him. "Have you honestly captured Raggedy Andy and the Snitznoodle?"

"Honest!" Hookie replied. "And I have put Raggedy Andy in a trunk and the Snitznoodle in a closet, and I have let all the air out of the rubber Howloon, and he is as flat and hungry as a pancake."

"Now I know that you are telling a fib," Raggedy Ann said. "For the Howloon is filled with cream puffs and cookies and lollypops. So he would not be that flat even if you did let all the air out of him!"

"Ha, ha!" the goblin laughed. "Just as soon as I let the air out of the Howloon, I saw that he was filled with something, so I snipped him open with my scissors and took out all the nice things."

Then Hookie went into his house and slammed the door behind him.

Presently Hookie's head poked from the window. "So you thought I was telling you a fib, did you, Miss Raggedy Ann? Just you look here!" and the mean little goblin dragged the Howloon to the window and threw him out. "Doesn't he look flat?"

Indeed! The poor Howloon was as flat as he had been in the cookie house.

"Yes he does!" Raggedy Ann replied. "And you should feel ashamed of yourself, Hookie-the-Goblin!"

"Well! I don't!" the goblin howled. But then, goblins do not feel ashamed as nice people do. So Raggedy Ann and her friends picked up the poor Howloon and carried him back into the bushes.

"We must patch him up right away," Raggedy Ann said. "Poor thing!"

"I shall run home and get the things for patching him," Mr. Cookie said, as he hastened towards the cookie house.

The cookie man also brought back cakes and cookies to stuff inside the rubber Howloon so that he would not feel hungry when he was patched. Raggedy Ann soon had him nicely mended, and then Little Weakie and Mr. Cookie pumped up the Howloon.

"I wouldn't be a goblin for anything!" the Howloon said when he could walk around.

"What can we do now?" Mr. Cookie wished to know.

The Howloon considered for a moment; then he said, "If there were some way for me to get in under the goblin's house, I could hump myself quickly, and upset it. Then you could all rush in and rescue our friends."

"There *is* a small hole beneath the goblin's house," Raggedy Ann said, "but it is much too small for you to crawl into."

"I'll tell you what you can do, Raggedy Ann," the Howloon declared when he saw how small the hole was. "You can take a pin and puncture me, then when all the wind is out of me, you can stuff me down into the small hole and pump me up!" So Raggedy Ann, knowing it would not hurt the Howloon, punctured him, and she and Mr. Cookie and Mrs. Cookie and Little Weakie all squeezed the wind out of him. When he was quite flat, they pushed the Howloon into the hole and all took turns pumping him up.

After they had pumped awhile, Raggedy Ann cried, "Look! It's making the goblin's house lean a way over sideways." This was quite true. The more air they pumped into the rubber Howloon, the more it tipped the goblin's house.

"What are you doing down there?" the goblin howled as he put his head out of the window. "The first thing you know you will tip my house over."

"That's just what we are going to do, Mr. Hookie," Raggedy Ann said. "Then we can rescue the Snitznoodle and Raggedy Andy."

"Better not pump any more," the Howloon called. "I am twice as large as I have ever been before, and I may pop like a toy balloon if I am blown too tight."

"Oh, dear!" Raggedy Ann said. "Just a little bit more and we would have tipped the goblin's house over. Let's all catch hold and pull!" So Raggedy Ann and Little Weakie and the cookie people all pulled at the goblin's house until it tipped right over. But, sad to relate, the house tipped so fast neither Raggedy Ann nor the cookie people nor the gingerbread man, nor Little Weakie had time to get out of the way and the house fell right on top of them.

When the house was down, Hookie put his head through the window. Then he climbed out. When he saw what had

happened he was delighted. He kicked his goblin heels in the air and howled with joy. "Aha, Raggedy Ann and all her friends are under the house and can't get out. So I have captured every last one of them!"

"Is that *so?*" a loud voice howled right behind the goblin. And there stood the Howloon. For, when the house tipped over, he was not under it any more. He was all covered with spider webs and dried leaves and sticks, so he did not look anything like himself. And then, too, he was twice as large as he had ever been before.

Hookie turned about, and when he saw this large, strange-looking creature he scampered away through the woods as fast as he could go.

The Howloon went to the goblin's shed and found a long iron bar. Then he placed a stone near the house, and with the long iron bar resting on the stone, he was able to raise the goblin's house so his friends could crawl out. The Howloon took the iron bar and punched the iron door until the hinges broke. And Raggedy Ann lost no time in climbing in the house and unlocking the trunk.

Then she and Raggedy Andy unlocked the closet door and rescued the nice Snitznoodle.

Everyone was glad that everything had turned out so nicely.

They laughed and chatted as they walked through the woods towards the cookie home, for they knew Mrs. Cookie would prepare a nice dinner as soon as they reached home.

So they all caught hold of hands and ran to get up a good appetite. But, when they reached the cookie house, what was their surprise to find the door locked.

"Dear me," Mrs. Cookie exclaimed. "I did not lock the door."

"Well, it is locked now!" Raggedy Andy said.

CHAPTER TEN

THE LAST OF THE GOBLIN'S TRICKS

INDEED, the candy door of the cookie house was locked and our friends knew pretty well that Hookie-the-Goblin was the one who had locked it.

Raggedy Andy walked up to the candy door and knocked, *thump, thump.*

"What do you want? Nobody is at home," the goblin cried through the candy key hole.

"Oh, what a fib!" Raggedy Andy said. "We can hear you walking around inside, Hookie-the-Goblin."

"I sha'n't let you in," the Goblin shouted.

"You open this door right away, Mr. Hookie, or I'll come in and wrestle you," Raggedy Andy cried.

"Yes, and I'll come in and give you a hard thump," the Snitznoodle added.

"Ha, ha, ha!" the goblin laughed. "Come right in then. Let me see you do it! I have the door locked, and I shall not open it until I am ready."

"I just know that Hookie will spoil everything in our house," Mrs. Cookie said. "He will eat up all the cakes, then he will nibble all the candy icing from the chairs and everything."

"I suppose he will nibble even the candy covered cookie organ," the Snitznoodle said. "Goblins are such silly creatures."

"Oh! I know what let's do!" the Howloon suggested. "Let's tip the cookie house over just as we did the goblin's house, then when Hookie comes running out, Raggedy Andy can wrestle him, and the Snitznoodle can give him a few thumps."

"We can't do that!" decided Raggedy Ann. "For, if we tip over the cookie house, we shall break all the candy shingles and all the candy furniture, and ruin everything in the house."

"No," Raggedy Andy agreed, "we cannot tip over the cookie house for that would break everything, and the nice cookie people would have no place to live."

"Then," the Howloon said, "I shall run back to the goblin's shed and get an iron bar I saw there and with that I shall break in the candy door. It will be easy to make another once we get inside the house."

"That is a good plan," Mr. Cookie said.

"Yes," Mrs. Cookie agreed, "I have lots of cake dough and I can easily bake another door and cover it with molasses candy."

"All right," the Howloon cried. "I will get the iron bar. It will only take me a few minutes. Then we shall get into the cookie house and chase the goblin out for good."

So the Howloon ran through the woods after the iron bar.

Raggedy Ann and the cookie people and Little Weakie and Raggedy Andy and the nice, kind Snitznoodle waited and waited for the Howloon to return. But when they had waited ever and ever so long, and the Howloon did not come back, Raggedy Ann said, "Maybe the Howloon has for-

gotten what he went after and has stopped to take a nap. I will run to the goblin's house and see what is keeping him."

When Raggedy Ann reached the goblin's house, first she heard a shrill whistle, and it grew louder and louder until, she could hear the Howloon inside the goblin's shed making the most awful racket by howling. And a Howloon can howl almost as loud as a steam engine can whistle when a Howloon wishes to howl. Raggedy Ann ran to the shed. There she found that the Howloon had stepped inside, the door had closed behind him, and there he was, locked in.

Once he was out, the Howloon picked up the long iron bar saying: "Now I shall take you upon my back, Raggedy Ann, and run back to the cookie house, and punch down the candy-covered door."

So Raggedy Ann climbed upon the Howloon's back, and rode back to the cookie house.

When the Howloon and Raggedy Ann reached the cookie house, none of their friends were in sight. "Oh dear!" Raggedy Ann cried, as she noticed this, "I am afraid the goblin has captured them again!"

But the goblin had not captured Raggedy Andy and the Snitznoodle and Little Weakie and the nice cookie people as Raggedy Ann supposed.

Instead, after Raggedy Ann had gone to the goblin's house to find the Howloon, Raggedy Andy and the Snitznoodle and Little Weakie and the cookie people sat down to wait for Raggedy Ann and the Howloon to return. And in a short time, the goblin came to the door and threw it wide open.

"Ha, ha, ha!" he cried, "that's the time I fooled you, Raggedy Andy!"

"Ha, ha, ha! How did you fool me, Mr. Hookie-the-Goblin? Just tell me that."

"Why," the goblin cried as he came outside, "you thought that I intended to remain a mean old goblin all my life, and that I should not let you or the cookie people inside their house, didn't you?"

"That is what we thought," Raggedy Andy said.

"Well! that's how I fooled all of you. You see," the goblin explained, "I decided that it wasn't any fun teasing and capturing you all the time. And I found out that being mean to others, just made it seem as though everyone was being mean to me. So, when you tipped my house over, I knew it served me right, for I had been mean to all of you.

"And when I ran over here, I said to myself, 'Mr. Hookie-Goblin, the best thing for you to do is to change from a mean old goblin into a good goblin. And the best way to do that is to do something nice for the Raggedys and the cookie people and the Snitznoodle and Little Weakie and the Howloon.'"

"But do you think it was nice to run into the cookie people's house without even knocking, and then lock the door so that they could not get in?" Raggedy Andy asked.

"Oh, no!" the goblin laughed. "I know it is not polite to go into people's houses when they are not at home. But I thought to myself, 'Now, the cookie people and the Raggedys and Little Weakie and the Snitznoodle and the Howloon will be very hungry when they return. So I will just slip inside and set the table, and pull up the chairs, and fix a nice dinner, and have everything ready when they return.'

"And that is just what I did. But you hurried so fast I didn't have time to do all I planned. So I had to wait until I had taken the cream puffs and the mince pie and the cake chicken from the oven. And now," the goblin laughed, "everything is ready and you can come in and have your dinner."

So everyone went inside, and there was a dinner just as nice as Mrs. Cookie or Raggedy Ann could have prepared it, and they all sat down in the candy chairs to eat. And, when Raggedy Ann and the Howloon came back and peeped in the window, that is where they found their friends.

So the Howloon and Raggedy Ann went inside and sat down, too.

"My!" Raggedy Ann said as she put a bib under the Howloon's chin, "I am so glad the goblin has changed into a nice goblin."

"So am I," Hookie-the-Goblin laughed, "for now I shall always live with the cookie people and be their hired girl."

And even though Mrs. Cookie tried to tell the goblin that she liked to do the work, the goblin would not sit at the table with them. "No, sir!" he said. "I have decided that it is lots more fun doing for others than having others do for you. So from now on I wish to be the hired girl and wait on the table and brush the crumbs away and shoo the chickens off the porch just like Orphan Annie!"

So after dinner Raggedy Ann and all the others baked cookie-and-cake-bricks and built another bedroom for Hookie-the-Goblin so that he could always live at the cookie house.

The Howloon, of course, could sleep in the same room with the Snitznoodle because the Snitznoodle did not snore. Howloons hardly ever snore except when their rubber sides get punctured, and that is hardly a snore. It's more of a whisper.

So Raggedy Ann and Raggedy Andy stayed at the cookie house for a few days because, now that the goblin was a nice goblin, everyone could have so much fun.

Then, one night, when all the others were asleep except Raggedy Ann, she rose up in bed and woke Raggedy Andy. "We must return to the nursery, Raggedy Andy," she said. "And I cannot bear to tell our nice friends good-bye. We shall write a note and leave it on the kitchen table where they will find it the very first thing in the morning."

So Raggedy Ann scratched a note upon three candy covered cookies and left them upon the kitchen table. Then she and Raggedy Andy tiptoed from the cookie house and ran to the grotto.

The Raggedys had a little fun sliding for a while upon the ice floor. But they knew they must not spend too much time there.

They wished that they might take some of the soda water icicles home to Uncle Clem, Frederika, Henny, and the other dolls, but soda water icicles melt too easily.

At last Raggedy Andy discovered the steps leading up from the grotto, and soon the two rag dolls had come out of the ground, and were scampering across the fields towards their nursery home.

"Well, Mr. Raggedy Andy," Raggedy Ann whispered as they climbed into their two little beds, "didn't we have a nice adventure?"

And Raggedy Andy, his little bright shoe button eyes shining up at the ceiling, whispered back, "Indeed! we did, Raggedy Ann. And won't the other dolls be surprised when we tell them of it in the morning?"

95